S0-BNH-919

THE DEATH
OF
DESERT BELLE

THE DEATH
OF
DESERT BELLE

•

Phil Dunlap

AVALON BOOKS
NEW YORK

PRINTED IN THE UNITED STATES OF AMERICA
ON ACID-FREE PAPER
BY HADDON CRAFTSMEN, BLOOMSBURG, PENNSYLVANIA

This book is dedicated to my wife, Judy, whose faith has been my inspiration, and to my family and friends who encouraged and supported my thirst for writing about the mysterious Old West.

Chapter One

Shortly after dawn in the dusty Arizona hamlet of Desert Belle, a thin cloud of dust hovered in the still, hot air like an open umbrella. An explosion several hours earlier in the middle of a stifling July night had leveled the back half of the old adobe jail, spewing dust and debris two hundred feet in the air. That early morning found many of the town's seventy-five residents milling about, gawking and supposing.

Merchants stopped at the site to speculate as to the probable cause, none daring to prod a pensive sheriff for particulars as he stood knee-deep in rubble. The deep frown on the lawman's face made it clear he wasn't in the mood to answer questions from the curious. He surveyed the damage with his deputy as they scratched about in the midst of what little remained of the building.

An empty ore wagon rattled to a stop in the middle of the street. The two men aboard studied the scene for only a minute. The driver just shook his head, then leaned over and spat a dark stream of tobacco juice into the street as the other shifted uncomfortably, mumbling something about being glad he hadn't chosen that night to sleep one off in the jail.

Two ladies, passing by on their way to the dry goods emporium, clucked their tongues judgmentally, then hurried on lest they somehow become a part of whatever dreadful thing had happened during the early morning darkness.

1

The talk was that the notorious Bishop brothers had actually made good on their threat to escape before they could ever be brought to trial. Apparently, their gang had ridden into town in the middle of the night, placed a charge at the back of the jail and lit the fuse. Indeed, it *had* looked that way until two bodies were found crushed unrecognizably beneath the thick slabs of adobe wall and heavy beams blown apart by the blast. The two men with badges stood shaking their heads.

"Marshal Kelly brought them in; best get a telegraph off to let him know there's no need to be comin' back for a trial. He's probably still over in Ft. Huachuca," Sheriff Rufus Potter said to his deputy. He crossed his arms and sighed at the results of what appeared to have been enough dynamite to open Yuma Prison.

"Damned shame. Too bad the Bishops had to die like this before we could watch 'em stretch hemp," the sheriff lamented.

Deputy Ben Satterfield scratched around in the rubble with an iron bar. He poked at a hinge blown off the heavy plank door that had separated the jail from the sheriff's office, the only part of the building left standing. A splintered door lay flat beneath adobe bricks. Large cracks threatened to collapse the back wall of the office itself unless something was done quickly to shore it up.

"Makes a body wonder, don't it, Sheriff?"

"Wonder? Wonder 'bout what?" Sheriff Potter mumbled. The ambivalence in his voice left small doubt as to his lack of interest in the deputy's speculations. He continued to shuffle through the debris where a cell had stood only hours before, occupied by two of the territory's most notorious criminals. The sheriff moved about with slow deliberation. His scuffed and worn boots were run down in the heels from both his weight and his slightly bowlegged posture.

Undaunted by the sheriff's cool response, deputy Satterfield continued, "Them Bishops has been blowin' up bank safes for more'n a dozen years. And they always seem to end up with what they're aimin' for without blastin' away half a building to get it."

"But it wasn't the Bishops themselves did the blowin' up this time. Hell, there's no tellin' how many sticks those fools might have used," Potter said with a wave of his hand, his puffy cheeks flushed with impatience at Satterfield's incessant supposings.

"Maybe so, but you'd think they'd learned a darn sight more about explosives from all the times they used it when Ord and Hale Bishop were callin' the shots," Satterfield continued undaunted.

"What is it you're tryin' to say, Ben?"

"Oh, nothin', I reckon. Jus' seems strange they picked this time to get careless, needin' to get their leaders free an' all," Ben said, tossing the bent piece of iron back into the debris. The bar rang as it struck the rocky floor. "I'll just get that telegraph off to the marshal like you said."

"You do that; an' while you're at it, suppose you quit worryin' about whether or not the Bishops rode with a bunch of fools. It's done an' that's that."

The sheriff stood for a moment watching after the deputy, who quickly crossed the street and disappeared into the telegraph office a half block down. Satterfield hadn't brought up anything that wasn't common knowledge. The Bishop gang *was* known for their unique abilities with explosives, with many successes.

He just mumbled incoherently as he turned his attention back to the mess that lay around him. He kicked at a piece of adobe brick that lay near his boot, then ambled off toward the mayor's office to see about getting the jail rebuilt as soon as possible. For a time, he'd have to hold any prisoners in the miner's storehouse—the only other building in Desert Belle that offered any reasonable security. At least it was built of heavy timbers, with substantial padlocks on the doors of two windowless rooms. It would have to suffice until the town council approved the money to get the jail reconstructed, an ordeal he dreaded.

The money would have to come mostly from the pockets of storekeepers, and none of those pockets were very deep. For no apparent reason, the once prosperous town had suffered from a business slump for the past couple of years. The sheriff's fears of coming up short of cash to rebuild were well founded.

The bodies of the two notorious brothers wouldn't be placed on display in front of the undertaker's parlor because they were so badly mangled by the force of the explosion that their bodies were unrecognizable. The two were buried as quickly as a grave could be dug.

"Hey, Littlejohn, wake up! I need to send a telegraph, *pronto*," Satterfield said as he stomped into the untidy office of the telegrapher, Asa Littlejohn. A spindly, balding man, with spectacles that had slipped half-way down his thin nose, Asa was shaken from his mid-morning snooze by the sound of Satterfield's booming voice.

"Don't have to scare a body to death, Satterfield," Asa muttered, removing his feet from his cramped desk. He rubbed his eyes as he unwound his gangly legs to arrive in a sitting position. "What's so gosh-darned important that you have to come bargin' in here like a bull in a china shop?"

"Sheriff sent me to stop Marshal Kelly from comin' all the way back here for the Bishop's trial, since there ain't no more need for one. Or so it's claimed. Give me something to write on."

"What d'you mean by that?" Littlejohn asked, as he shuffled through a collection of papers, records, and two dime novels in search of a pencil. Finding a stub, he handed it to Ben along with a small scrap of paper.

"Nothin', I reckon. Just that it all seems strange them boys'd mess up so bad they kill their own." Ben touched the point of the pencil to his tongue and began scratching out his message. After a few hasty scribbles, he handed the paper to Asa.

"Well, it ain't our worry no more. Best just put it out of your mind. Now if you'll quit jawin', I'll get this message off," Asa said as he pulled the telegraph key closer. With a deft touch, he began to tap out the scrawled words Satterfield had written. As he got near the end, he stopped. "You sure you want to add this last part, Ben? Sheriff might be a little put out."

Ben nodded. "Send her, Asa." He waited to be sure the message went as he instructed, then turned and lumbered through the door. Asa returned to his former position, nearly guaranteeing a resumption of his nap within minutes.

Ben Satterfield had been a deputy for ten years. He had been passed over for sheriff three times. In fact, he probably never would be the town's choice for sheriff as long as King Slaughter owned the biggest mining operation in the area. Slaughter would rather see Satterfield dead.

Just over two years back, Ben had been forced to gun down Slaughter's son when the younger Slaughter got roaring drunk and shot up the town, killing a young mother as she tried to cross the street to get her children to safety when the shooting started. Two horses tied to a hitching rail also went down in the hail of bullets. When the deputy arrived, young Slaughter was raving and shooting wildly at anything and everything. He refused to surrender when confronted by the deputy, and Satterfield saw no recourse but to put an end to the young man's spree in defense of the town. After giving the youth every opportunity to call a halt to the carnage, the deputy saw it ending only one way—with a bullet.

King never forgave the deputy. In Slaughter's eyes, his boy was just a little wild, but no more so than any young mustang, and letting off steam was natural for an eighteen-year-old. To Ben, it wasn't the age of the shooter that made a difference, it was the damage being done by the youth's brace of Remington .44s. And Ben saw it as his job to put a stop to any further carnage and property damage. He did his job.

It was probably just as well that the overweight, unkempt deputy would never rise to higher office, as he had little stomach for the politics involved. He wanted nothing more than to be left alone to do his job—a job that let him avoid having to kiss the boots of the mayor and the town council.

The sheriff wasn't so lucky. He was the third man to hold the office since the town was started in '68. However, each preceding sheriff had chosen to keep Satterfield on as deputy because no one knew the town like Ben. Besides, the town council actually liked the deputy. For all his rough edges and slovenly behavior, Ben Satterfield was a good lawman—just not sheriff material. He had the respect of all who knew him— all except King Slaughter, and—perhaps, Potter.

"Sheriff, I'm takin' on a powerful hunger. It's about time for lunch, and I'm thinkin' of goin' over to the cafe. You mind?" Ben said as he entered the small office that was left standing. He looked around at the disarray and thick covering of dust on everything. He wasn't eager to help with the clean-up. Feeding his stomach seemed a better choice.

"Naw, you go ahead. I'll stick around 'til you get back," Sheriff Potter mumbled, never looking up from the mess that surrounded him.

The sheriff erupted with a loud sneeze, then returned to tidying up what he could. Dust swirled about with his every move. He drew a handkerchief from his back pocket and tied it across his face, hoping to breath as little of the fine dust as possible.

Sheriff Rufus Potter had been sheriff of four different towns before he came to Desert Belle. A short, stocky man in his forties, Potter was the perfect politician. With an uncanny ability to bend whichever way the partisan winds blew, he somehow managed to side with the majority, thus avoiding an ignominious defeat at the polls every two years.

Considering his propensity for staying in favor with those in power, many held an unvoiced curiosity as to why he'd lost three other jobs as sheriff before settling in an out–of–the–way scrub-tree town like Desert Belle. They all wondered, but questions came to nothing more than speculations over whiskey at the Shot-to-Hell Saloon.

Today, however, the conversations were more apt to concern the bungled escape attempt. There would be more than a few shaking heads and smug snickers. Most would freely voice their opinions that justice had finally taken its proper course. Drinks might even be on the house—at least the first round.

Chapter Two

U.S. Marshal Piedmont Kelly was standing outside the officer's quarters talking to Cavalry Captain John Braxton when the telegraph message arrived at Ft. Huachuca. The wide overhang of the tin-roofed porch that ran the length of the adobe building shaded the two from the early afternoon sun. From across the parade ground the rhythmic clanging of the blacksmith's hammer echoed off the buildings. Just outside one of the barracks, a handful of raw recruits stood in a ragged line as a sergeant bellowed orders that seemed largely ignored. Nearby, a young cavalryman walked his lathered mare after a workout, the side-to-side slapping of the horse's tail keeping cadence as they went.

"Marshal, this here's for you, Sir," an out-of-breath young trooper said as he ran up. He snapped to attention, saluted the captain, then slapped the paper into the marshal's outstretched hand and hurried off without another word.

"Thank you, trooper," Kelly called after him. He unfolded the paper, scanned it quickly, then—not wishing to exclude the captain—read the message aloud. "Bishop Brothers blown up in escape attempt. No trial forthcoming as both dead. Have my own doubts, however. Deputy B. Satterfield. Desert Belle, Arizona Territory."

With a look of concern, the young marshal stroked his bushy mustache with his index finger for a moment, then slowly refolded the paper and stuffed it into his vest pocket. "Hmmm. Wonder what he means by 'having doubts'. If he said it to raise my curiosity, he got the job done. Reckon I better ride to Desert Belle and have a look."

"I've known Ben for years and I've never known him to be cryptic. I'd be curious, too," Captain Braxton said. "But, when you're dead, you're dead. That's the plain and simple of it. What's there to doubt?"

"Let's hope he's just confused. But I can't afford any confusion over whether or not the Bishops might still be around to terrorize the citizenry. If you should get wind of anything, you'll find me in Desert Belle."

"Okay, Marshal," Braxton nodded, with a look of surrender. He then turned on his heel and strode across the parade ground with the confident air of a veteran cavalry officer.

Kelly went straight to his spartan quarters to gather a few necessities for his ride to Desert Belle: a freshly boiled shirt, extra socks, shaving soap and razor, and his last half-empty box of .44 caliber center–fire cartridges for his revolver. He'd have to pick up more cartridges for his Winchester before leaving. He tugged at the short, dark curtains that covered the solitary window of his room in order to let enough light in to locate his saddle bags and bedroll which hung over the back of the room's only chair, an ancient and unsteady ladder-back long overdue for conversion to kindling.

He stopped as he came to a folded wanted poster that had found its way to the bottom of one of his saddle bags. He unfolded the poster to a shiver of anger as he stared into the eyes of the Bishops looking back at him from the wrinkled paper. His mind raced back to the ordeal of capturing the Bishop brothers less than a month earlier in a bloody shootout which had left two cavalry troopers dead, a third wounded. They were not pleasant memories.

The two Bishop brothers, along with one other member of their gang, had robbed a stagecoach carrying—among other things—a federal payroll bound for Ft. Huachuca. An army patrol had come upon the seemingly deserted coach, finding the driver, guard, and one passenger dead. They returned to

Ft. Huachuca with two surviving passengers, both women, found uninjured except for severe exposure. The outlaws had left them to fend for themselves by whatever means they could find, an act that could easily result in a death sentence in this hostile country.

Soon after the stage had been found, rumors began to surface that the Bishops were holed up in the hills west of Tombstone, in an area near the long-abandoned Indian village of Santa Cruz.

Going after the murderous gang had fallen to Marshal Kelly, because there was a federal payroll on board. And, as that payroll was meant for troops at Ft. Huachuca, Captain Braxton also insisted the army had an obligation to get involved in its recovery, and to take whatever means were necessary to ensure the safe return of the contents of the army strongbox.

So, he assembled a patrol to accompany the tough, young marshal. Kelly soon found himself faced with the prospect of eight armed and over-eager young soldiers accompanying him in tracking and capturing those responsible for the robbery. It was help he didn't want, and hadn't asked for. A handful of green troopers would bring him no advantage over the Bishops. More likely just the opposite. But the situation was such—with the payroll having been meant for the very troops he'd be riding with—that he felt obliged to go along with the captain's insistence. The circumstances warranted a spirit of cooperation. Since he never knew when the time might come he'd welcome a troop of cavalry, he kept his real concerns to himself. He remembered well the conversation with Braxton that day.

"Captain, there really isn't any need for troops. There's only three of 'em. I'll have 'em back here in a week or less."

"Sorry, Kelly, I've got too much at stake to take any chances on them three getting away with our money. If I don't do something, the men will think I'm not rightly concerned about their pay. Can't let that happen. My troopers are going along and that's that."

"Okay, but if I can't change your mind, at least send one

of your scouts along with the troop. They know those hills better than any of your officers."

"I'll be needing all the scouts I have to accompany a troop going after Black Skull. That damned Apache's been raiding ranches in the area again. The squad will have to make do on their own."

Kelly shook his head and moved off toward the soldiers gathering in front of a barracks. They were nearly ready to ride out as he came up to Lieutenant Graber, who had been put in charge.

"I'll be with you as soon as I pick up some ammunition, Lieutenant," Kelly said.

"Don't be long, Marshal," Graber said, "we're moving out in precisely ten minutes, with or without you."

"No need to be in a hurry, son. Riding headlong into pitched gun battle against experienced gunmen isn't something to look forward to." Kelly continued past the troopers, whose attention he now had. "And a battle is something you can count on with this bunch."

"We'll be ready," Graber said with certainty. Kelly nodded as he continued to the quartermaster's office.

The marshal knew he wasn't obligated to even ride with the troopers. They weren't under his command. Nor was he under the young lieutenant's. But he took it into his head to ride along with them, as long as they didn't get in the way of a successful capture of the Bishops.

A few hours from the fort, near where the stagecoach had been found, the troopers easily picked up the Bishops' trail and zealously began following it into the hills. To the young lieutenant, the trail looked as if the Bishops were in too much of a hurry to cover their tracks, possibly fearful of army pursuit. To Kelly, it looked like a trail left by someone who wanted to be followed—right into a trap.

This wasn't the first time the outlaw gang had led pursuers into those same hills. Numerous tricky switchbacks, deeply eroded ravines, and steep sandstone cliffs offered a wealth of opportunities for an ambush.

Ord and Hale Bishop knew the land as well as the Apaches,

and better than most soldiers or lawmen. They plundered the Arizona and New Mexico territories at will, keeping far to the south so that they might easily slip across the border into Mexico just in case some potential captor got too close, however unlikely.

Lieutenant Graber ordered his men to follow wherever the trail led, against Kelly's best advice. That advice suggested following an outlaw's trail too closely could get someone killed. Men on the run fought best hiding behind rocks or in crevices, keeping company with the snakes and scorpions— other desert inhabitants whose deadly attacks came without warning. Outlaw kin.

Since the marshal had no authority over the army, the best he could do was give advice. The stubborn lieutenant's decision to ignore that advice left Marshal Kelly no choice but to pursue the gang his own way. So, after only one day, he left the trail, and the troopers, to follow his own plan.

Kelly thought to circle around the desert flats and take the high ground in hopes of discovering the Bishops waiting below—like the desert tarantula waits, rock-still, for an unwary victim to blunder into its trap. The Bishops would stay down amongst the boulders and mesquite and dry creek beds, avoiding any chance of being seen silhouetted against the intensely blue sky.

Kelly headed for the top, a difficult and dangerous undertaking, but he knew the Bishops would take the easy way out. The problem for the cavalry troop was that their lieutenant chose the same route as the Bishops, making them easy targets for the outlaw gang that might be awaiting them from any number of perfect hiding places. The troopers wouldn't stand a chance.

Making his way over some of the most hostile terrain, Kelly pushed his gelding to its limits. The heaving animal strained to climb shale-strewn hillocks, weaving around sharply-faceted boulders as large as houses, stepping warily to avoid snake or prairie dog holes.

The marshal's strategy paid off as he topped a jagged ridge just above a sharp bend in the trail. The perfect trap. He spotted the three outlaws only moments before the shooting started. Nearly too late.

The soldiers had been caught in a box canyon with no cover, no way to maneuver, and little chance for escape, except to scrape their bellies on the rocky desert floor and try to shoot their way out.

By the time the marshal was able to get into a position that would let him throw down on the outlaws, two troopers lay dead, with a third badly wounded. With his Winchester cocked and ready, Piedmont Kelly stepped boldly into a narrow opening behind the outlaws—their only avenue of escape—and with his move, the odds in the game changed dramatically. He ordered the Bishops to throw down their weapons.

Realizing their untenable position, Ord and Hale were smart enough to quickly comply. The third man, a hardcase named K. D. Keyes, decided to test the reputed lightning speed of this marshal with the Winchester. Keyes lost.

The marshal herded the Bishops off to the nearest town with a jail, Desert Belle. There, he left them in the custody of Sheriff Potter to await trial for their crimes.

Since the stagecoach they robbed was civilian, the army's responsibility ended when the payroll went back to Ft. Huachuca with the lieutenant. Kelly assumed the matter of the Bishop brothers' wanton plundering of the territory to be closed. They would be tried, found guilty, and most certainly hanged. No jury in a territory plagued with the viciousness of the Bishops' outlawry would consider freedom for the two. Justice was demanded.

Now this strange turn.

With all these events still fresh in his mind, and with a scowl on his face, Kelly strode to the corral to saddle his horse for the long ride to Desert Belle, all the while hoping Ben Satterfield was wrong.

Two troopers pulled open the wooden gates to let the marshal pass. Dust swirled about the big gelding's hooves with each step he took. Far off in the distance, dark clouds were forming over faintly visible mountains. There would soon be a giant thunderhead forming and a quick, violent storm would dump untold amounts of water in the higher elevations, water which would quickly find its way down to the desert floor, flooding dry creek beds with a raging flash flood. But the life-giving waters would soak rapidly into the parched sands, leaving wilderness creatures precious little time to get their share.

Kelly's two canteens sloshed a comforting sound as the gelding trotted away from the fort, and toward a mystery.

Chapter Three

It was true; Zebulan A. Pooder *did* have the look of a pig farmer. Often, he even smelled like one. Today was no exception. Pooder, himself, naturally felt any such reference to his appearance insulting. And for that reason, a youthful defiance took charge of his soul on one fateful morning that found him standing in a rutted street in Charleston, Arizona Territory.

In spite of the heat, Pooder wore a long, tan, trail duster over bib overalls rolled up at the bottom, square-toed shoes worn nearly through, and a frayed, sweat-stained straw hat the tattered brim of which drooped forlornly. His clothes were filthy from his being on the trail for weeks. To this farm boy's way of thinking, a bath somewhere along the way was out of the question, mainly because of the lack of ten cents to pay for a copper tub full of hot water and a bar of soap.

It was nine a.m., just before the sun began to reach its midday intensity.

"Hey, pig farmer, if you'd use the back entrance to town, you'd stand a better chance of staying downwind of us decent folk," said a loud, disagreeable cowboy leaning against a porch railing.

The man doing all the bellowing was Eb Johanson, an unemployed low-life who always managed to show up well-heeled after each of his many absences from town. No one who valued his life ever openly questioned how he seemingly could do nothing day after day, yet peel off greenbacks for drinks like an eastern banker whenever he wished.

On this particular day he'd taken a keen dislike to the shaggy-haired, seventeen-year-old boy from Kentucky who'd ridden into town with a friend the day before.

The boy had come to Arizona to find something better than breaking his back on a hard-clay farm in Kentucky. While his long journey across the frontier had been arduous, he'd seen no day so bad as to give him reason to miss the travails he'd left. Today was shaping up to be the exception.

In an attempt to ignore the man confronting him, Pooder slapped the reins of his horse over the hitching rail. He then turned to his companion and nodded his head as an instruction for him to do the same.

The young boy with Pooder, remaining astride a white-faced mule despite Pooder's signal to follow him in dismounting, was Blue LeBeau, a mulatto from Mississippi with whom Pooder had met up on the trail through Texas. Blue was running away from his own kind of adversity.

Blue's French father was a landowner of small means not far from Natchez. His mother, a free-born woman of color, had spent her life taking care of Blue and his father on a nearly worthless, rock-strewn cotton farm.

Often ridiculed for his strange name, Blue had been forced to tell time and again how he came to be saddled with such a moniker. The day he was born, he related, he had been wrapped in a gunny sack with indigo printing on the sides. Some of the ink came off on his moist skin, leaving an image. Even though the blue stain washed off immediately, the inspiration of what to name him came instantly. Blue! His mother saw it as some sort of sign from heaven.

One winter, Blue's mother fell victim to a fever and died. His distraught father began drinking heavily and taking his anger out on Blue. So, in an ill-considered act of rebellion against the brutality bestowed on him by the sodden old man, fifteen-year-old Blue lit out for the western frontier to find the illusive magical ore about which his mother had filled his young head: Gold.

"You boys ever seen a real gunfighter?" Johanson asked, pointing a long, bony finger in Pooder's direction. "I'll bet a dime to a dollar you ain't." Dark, deep-set eyes narrowed as he took one quick step toward the youth.

Pooder made a hasty decision to hold his ground as he answered with youthful defiance, "Have so, lots of times."

"I think you're a lying heap of bull dung! Takes a real man to handle one of these," Johanson said, patting the Remington .44 on his hip. "And I aim to show you a real one in action, the first and certainly the last one you'll ever see."

He glanced around to see how many of the curious he'd attracted by his antics. Being the center of attention had become a career for the hardcase who'd bragged about killing several men, though no one in Charleston had ever seen him do it.

At Johanson's words, a chill went up Pooder's spine. He blurted out, "I ain't even got a holster, mister. Who'd shoot a boy too poor to own a holster?"

"Pull back that coat and let's take a look see. Only a fool'd be out in this country with no gun."

With hands thrust deeply into the large patch pockets of his soiled duster, Pooder pulled open the coat like giant bat wings.

"See? No holster, just like I said."

"Well you are a fool, and fools need to be taught a lesson," the gunman admonished. He'd lost his mocking smirk.

Johanson motioned to one of the several dirt-weary miners who'd stopped to see what he was up to. "Toliver, lay your hogleg at the feet of this miserable excuse for a man."

A toothless, scruffy old man stepped away from the group, drew his revolver from its holster, then, laying it in the dirt in front of the boy, hurried back to stand on the boardwalk with the others.

The weapon the man had laid in the street was a war-vintage Colt that had not been converted to the more common center-fire cartridges. The old revolver probably hadn't even been fired in years.

Pooder glanced at the tired, rusty thing lying there, his mind racing. He knew the man facing him was pushing him to defend himself in a fight that wasn't of his making. He didn't even know this man or what had him so upset. Except for an involuntary shiver, he made no attempt to move, nor did he remove his hands from the pockets of his duster. He had every right to be in Charleston. Just stand firm, he told himself. He felt his skin tingle at the thought. He needed time to think this situation over, but time was getting scarcer by the moment. His heart was pounding like a stamping mill. Whump. Whump. Whump.

"Unless you've a mind to let me use you for target practice, I'd say you'd best go for that gun lyin' at your feet." Johanson took a stance and placed his hand near the butt of the gun at his side. "I'll give you a chance to pick it up, then on the count of three, I'm gonna put a bullet in you whether you've filled your hand or not."

Finally Pooder spoke, trying to hide the shake in his voice. "Look, I ain't got nothing against you, mister, and I ain't done nothing to get you so riled up. We're just looking to go into the store and get some grub. Then we'll be on our way."

The boys had been camping just outside of town for a couple of days and were tired, near starved, and down to their last few pennies. They had come here in hopes of finding work. They had been trying to get on with one of the mines, though neither of them had even a lick of experience. The last three foremen laughed them off the premises.

"I told you yesterday to git. So, now you're gonna get the chance to show you got the guts to face me down, or hightail it right now. And no supplies is goin' with you."

Pooder didn't move. He wasn't sure just why, but he stood his ground. Blue, noticeably nervous over the situation, remained seated on the white-faced mule, tugging unconsciously at his faded and frayed gallowses. Suddenly, he leaned down and whispered something to Pooder that Johanson couldn't hear. The outlaw's disposition grew even nastier as the boys exchanged whispers.

He barked, "Hey, farmer, tell that young fool with you he'd

better move on outta here now because when I'm finished with you, he's next!"

Pooder's face flushed and his eyes narrowed at the man's words. As if frozen in place, he made no move, either for the gun laying at his feet or for his horse.

Johanson began to slowly slip his .44 from its holster. "Not many men get to name the time they're going to die. Where'd you like it?" he asked.

"Wherever you think is right," Pooder blurted out defiantly, the words almost catching in his dry throat.

"Bein' gut shot is slow and painful, just what a mangy drifter like you deserves. Last chance." He brought the gun up to waist level and thumbed back the hammer. A cruel smirk formed on his weather-etched face.

The onlookers were all startled by the sound of the shot.

Whaam!

With a look of total disbelief, Johanson slumped to his knees. His gun discharged harmlessly into the dirt as it fell from his hand. He fell forward, barely managing to turn his cheek as he landed hard on his face. He gasped and made a guttural growl of pain as dirt filled his mouth with each surging breath. He clutched his stomach with both hands, trying in vain to stem the spurting blood, his ashen face twisted in its search for what went wrong.

Pooder stood still, staring wide-eyed at the mortally wounded gunman, as a small wisp of smoke drifted up from the hole in his duster pocket. His hand still clung tightly to an unseen .32 caliber spur-trigger pocket pistol.

"I-I'm sorry, mister. Damn! Why'd you have to keep pushing?" he said, shaking as he tried to dismiss the fear gripping his insides. Sweat broke out on his face, leaving a dirty trail as it ran down his forehead.

Several onlookers ran to where Johanson lay. Constable James Burnett started off the step in front of his office and sauntered toward Pooder.

"It-it was self-defense, Constable," Pooder said, taking a halting step backward as he slowly withdrew his hands from his pockets and held them in the air, his wind-burned face turned pasty white.

"I know, I know. You can put 'em down. I seen the whole thing. Sooner or later it was bound to happen. That dumb Swede never knew when to keep his big mouth shut. Of course, I reckon them boys he rides with ain't gonna see it quite that way. If I was you, I'd skedaddle outta here before they get wind of this and show up with half a dozen more just like this one."

The Constable stood over Johanson shaking his head. "Somebody see if you can locate Doc Smith, although I don't see it doin' much good. Never seen a gut-shot man live for more than a couple days, usually no more than a few hours."

Pooder shivered at the thought.

Blue LeBeau finally dismounted and tugged at Pooder's sleeve. "That constable's right, best we get outta town. C'mon!"

Pooder pulled away with a frown. "We ain't goin' nowhere until we get what we come for."

"We can get them supplies over in Millville, across the river. C'mon," Blue pleaded.

Pooder would have none of it. He strode purposefully into the general store without looking back. He was feeling a kind of strange, frightened pride at what he'd just done.

Reluctantly, Blue followed at his heels. Blue had ridden with his older companion long enough to know there was no turning him once he had his mind set. Zeb Pooder was too stubborn for his own good, and Blue harbored a sick feeling that the incident wasn't finished.

As the two entered the general store, the proprietor followed them inside. He'd watched the whole incident from the liar's bench out front.

"Looks like you young fellers has cooked yourselves up a heap of trouble," he said, moving hurriedly around them to take up a position behind the counter. He adjusted his spectacles down low on his bony nose with a knowing squint.

"What do you mean?" Pooder asked.

"That fellow you shot rides with the Bishop gang."

Even with the door and windows open, the heat was becoming stifling in the heavily stocked room. At the revelation concerning Johanson, Pooder found himself overwhelmingly aware of the heat. He tried tugging at his collar for relief. Perspiration cascaded down his forehead.

"I heard the Bishops got killed," Blue said, eyes growing wide at the mention of the gang.

"Maybe so, maybe not. Don't make much difference either way. All the rest of that gang is still around and not far away, I hear tell."

The blood-drained look that arose almost instantly on the faces of the two boys was that of someone who'd just come face-to-face with a mountain lion. They turned to look at each other; then without further hesitation, bolted for the door. The goods they'd come for were still on the shelves.

Johanson's demand that Pooder leave empty-handed had become prophetic.

Chapter Four

Pooder and Blue stopped running their horses as soon as they lost sight of town. Although the sun was waning, the intense heat would have killed the heavily-lathered animals had the boys kept up their pace. The two reined in well off the trail behind a rocky, cactus-covered rise. With chests heaving, both animals were blowing and shaking their heads as their riders tried to calm them.

"Damn!" Blue cried out angrily as he tugged at the stomping mule's reins to completely bring the beast under control. "Damned if you didn't near get us both killed! That was a fool thing to do. Why didn't you just walk away? He gave you the opportunity!" He shook his head in disbelief at Pooder's foolishness.

"A man can't let himself be bullied. Why, my pa would roll over in his grave if he was to find out I skedaddled from a fight. Couldn't, I just couldn't."

"Hell was so close I could feel the devil's breath on my face. I didn't even know you had a gun, not till it roared to life, that is. I almost wet my pants, you blamed fool." Blue slapped the pommel of his saddle and looked away with a frown.

"Well, to tell the truth, I ain't had it for long. I sort of found it after I seen two gents duking it out in back of a saloon in Fort Worth. One of 'em lost it in the dirt, and he was too drunk to know, so I stuffed it in my pocket and went my merry way. That was two days before I met up with you. Only way I was to ever get my hands on a weapon. Good thing it still had bullets in it; I sure can't afford none of my own."

Pooder felt the need to ease Blue's anger. He didn't cotton to the idea of riding into the desert alone, trying to shake a band of pursuing outlaws. Even if his partner was only fifteen. He had never liked being alone. "I-I'm sorry, Blue. I didn't mean to scare you like that. But, you got to understand, I-I couldn't run. C'mon, we're friends, ain't we?"

That was really all Blue was looking for, an apology. An admission that someone gave a hoot about his opinion. He gave Pooder a forgiving nod and a weak smile.

"I reckon." Blue patted the calmed-down mule on the neck, drawing back a hand wet with foamy sweat.

"I wonder if that gang has already come lookin' for us like that store clerk said."

"Don't know, but we best move on," Blue said.

"Nope. We're turnin' back." Pooder climbed back on his horse.

"Back? You must be tetched! What if they're already on our trail?"

"First off, we need supplies. We ain't had nothin' to eat but hardtack and jerky since last Tuesday, and I'm gettin' darned hungry for a real meal," Pooder grumbled. He wasn't used to going for days without food. Even back home on that mud-hole of a farm, no one ever went hungry.

"What's the second reason?"

"To double back, and throw 'em off our trail. We'll make our way through them hills to the south towards Desert Belle." Pooder stood up in his stirrups drawing an imaginary map in the air, directing his plan like an army tactician.

"Oh, I see. Well, it still don't answer where we're gonna get some grub."

"Good thought. I ain't cogitated none on that yet. You got any ideas, Blue?"

"Well, we can't go back to town, that's for sure." He shook

his head slowly. The very thought of riding back into that potentially lethal situation made him sweat.

"Hmmm. Maybe we can at that," Pooder said, his face screwed up in deep thought. "Remember that livery stable right at the edge of town?"

"I remember . . . some. What about it?" Blue had paid no attention to the architecture. It wasn't buildings he was interested in, and he'd certainly had no time to take note of the scenery on their hasty trip out.

"Big and rickety, and some of the whipsaw sidin' was comin' off. There was a sign out front sayin' the owner was seekin' help. Now, if we was to sneak back into town right after dark, maybe the liveryman would stake us to some grub fer swampin' out the stalls tomorrow. We could stay inside and out of sight easy enough. Then, come the next mornin', we strike out."

"Sounds pretty risky to me. What if someone what seen you shoot that fellow brings his horse in or something, and goes and tells that gang?"

"I say we take the chance. You with me?"

"I-I dunno, I am mighty hungry, but—"

"But, nothin'. Come on. It'll be sundown before long and we want to get there before he shuts down the stable for the night."

Blue gave a reluctant sigh, then wheeled the white-faced mule around to follow his brash friend the long way back to town. They'd just have to make a little detour on their way to freedom. Blue was scared to go back, but he didn't want Pooder to think he was a coward. So, he went. But he wished at least he had a gun of his own.

Three members of the notorious Bishop gang rode into Charleston to inform Johanson that his talents were needed to accomplish a hold-up planned for a few days hence. As their horses stirred up dust along the wide street, the rider in the lead, Big Al Barton, spotted the dead body resting inside a pine casket in front of the carpenter's shop. Big Al's curiosity got the better of him and he pulled away from the others to

get a better look at the unfortunate soul. The grim agony of a
slow death from a stomach wound had changed Johanson's
appearance dramatically. His ashen gray features were twisted
into a gruesome death mask barely recognizable even by
friends. But Big Al Barton did recognize him.

"Abe! Bill! Over here," he yelled to the others who had
ridden on, oblivious to his leaving the group. "It's Johanson!
Somebody's killed him!"

The two others, Abel Short and Blackwater Bill DeMotte,
reined in their tired mounts, coaxed them about and rode
slowly back to where Big Al was gaping into the hastily constructed casket. They all stared at the corpse as if to deny the
reality of what they saw.

Abel leaned forward in the saddle, leaning hard on the pommel. He shook his head, then spat in the dust. He drew back
the reins and turned his horse back into the street. "Dumb
Swede," he mumbled under his breath. The others followed
as he headed for the nearest of the town's saloons seeking to
find out who killed Johanson.

All three of the men were wanted for various crimes, but
no one was particularly surprised to see them openly riding
down the main street of the bustling young town. Few even
turned to stare after them. After all, worse than these three
had ridden in on many occasions—men like Tom McLowery,
Ike Clanton, and John Ringo. The town of Charleston had
become accustomed to hardcases and cowboys from Tombstone and other wide-open towns across the San Pedro seeking
diversion from their usual hangouts. Besides, the law in
Charleston wasn't able to put up much resistance, therefore
posing little threat to their freedom.

Big Al Barton led the way into the Silver Strike Saloon,
pushing the door open with his left hand as his right rested
on the butt of his sidearm. Briefly letting their eyes adjust to
the dark interior, all three slowly scanned the room for anyone
who might be a threat to them, and, seeing none, they strode
confidently to the bar. Big Al led the way across the narrow
room, slapped a hand on the bar, and demanded of the bartender, "Who saw what happened to our friend, Johanson?"

Used to dealing with hardcases like these, the bartender eased down the bar toward the three, placed a glass he'd just dried in front of Barton and casually said, "Only that I hear he tried to face down a young drifter and he come out second best. That's all." The bartender pulled the cork from a half-filled bottle of amber-colored whiskey and started to pour Barton a drink.

Barton quickly placed his hand over the glass. "Got no time for that. Where's this drifter, now?" Barton demanded with a scowl.

The bartender re-corked the bottle and put it aside with a shrug. He wiped a wet spot with his towel and leaned his elbows on the bar. "Rode outta town, as far as I know."

Barton's eyes narrowed. He spun around to size up the small number of customers who sat scattered about the room talking and drinking, or playing cards.

"Do any of you know about this drifter that gunned down our friend?" he bellowed.

The room grew silent, but no one answered.

Big Al clumped heavily over to table where an old man sat nursing a nearly empty bottle of whiskey. Big Al grabbed the man roughly by his shirt collar, nearly yanking him out of his chair.

"Listen carefully, old man. I want to know which way that drifter went and I ain't got the patience to wait all day," he yelled in the old miner's face.

"I-I don't kn-know, sir. I didn't see n-nothin'," the wide-eyed man stammered. He was rewarded for his lack of knowledge by being shoved hard into his chair, nearly being tossed over backwards.

"Somebody better remember and darned quick, or I swear I'll burn this rat trap to the ground." He slowly turned his head, waiting for a response. His patience at an end, he pulled a match from his vest pocket and struck it on a table top as he leaned over to hold the flame near a dusty lace curtain that hung at one of the side windows. "This dump'll go up like dry kindlin'!"

"No need for that. They rode out into the hills to the north-west," came a raspy voice from out of the darkened rear of the room.

"They?" Big Al Barton growled, as he blew out the match and tossed the still smoking stub on the floor.

"There was two of 'em—just kids, really. They rode in to get supplies," came the answer. "Didn't come lookin' fer no trouble. Johanson had it comin'."

"Kids or no, they killed our friend and they'll pay just like any would," Abel Short called back over his shoulder, shaking his fist as the trio stormed out of the saloon.

From the rear of the saloon, the man who'd spoken scooted his chair back and stood up. He took one last swig from his glass, then replaced it on the table where he'd been sitting alone. He stepped to the front window and watched as the trio of hardcases headed straight for their horses. Sunlight streaming through the glass glinted off his constable's badge.

Once outside, Abel asked, "What do you figure on doin', Big Al?"

"Come early light, we'll head into them hills and track down them two. Can't be too hard to find, them bein' just kids and all. First though, we'll find some grub, then bed-down at the stable fer the night."

"Eatin' sounds good, but I ain't up to hittin' the sack just yet," Abel said.

"Sure, but I don't want you two gettin' yourselves so drunk you can't ride at sunup."

"Then you better come back to the saloon with us, just to make sure we don't go gettin' into no trouble, Mother Barton," Blackwater Bill said with a snicker.

"Maybe I will at that. A shot or two won't hurt me," Big Al said as Abel groaned and rolled his eyes. He'd seen plenty of times when just one drink had sent Big Al Barton into an angry rage.

He didn't have a reputation for holding his liquor well.

Chapter Five

Piedmont Kelly slumped wearily in the saddle as he rode into Desert Belle for the first time since capturing the notorious Bishop brothers nearly a month back. Now, after a long ride from Ft. Huachuca, the only thing on his mind was locating a bed for the night. It was nearly sundown as he rode past the hotel in hopes of finding a boarding house with cheaper accommodations.

As a U.S. Marshal he was reimbursed for travel expenses, but those funds were often slow in catching up to him when he was on the move. He was always on a tight budget, and watching every penny was imperative.

The town of Desert Belle looked as though it had been thrown together overnight. Windows rattled from the weight of passers-by on the rickety boardwalks, false fronts creaked at the smallest breeze. Only a half-dozen looked sturdy enough to actually inhabit.

At the end of Galt Street sat Nellie Dunham's, a lonely, two-story Queen Anne style house which showed signs of needing paint and repair. A small, rickety sign hung precariously beneath the porch roof proclaiming it to be the location of Dunham's Boarding House. Several of the rungs along the porch railing were missing like teeth out of an old comb.

As Kelly stepped up onto the creaky structure, he was greeted by a rosy-cheeked lady with pure white hair, a curly

27

wisp of which drooped out of place across her forehead. Out of habit, his hand shot up to remove his dusty Stetson as he smiled a weary hello.

"Evenin', Ma'am," he said. "I'll be needing a room for the night, maybe more, if you have a vacancy."

"Delighted to accommodate for as long as you need, Marshal. Six bits a night, breakfast and all the coffee you can put away. Evenin' meal's an extra two bits if you care to join us. But," she added, with a twinkle in her eye, taking quick notice of the Winchester rifle he carried, "no gunplay indoors." She slapped him on the back with a laugh, filling the air with a considerable trail dust.

Before stepping over the threshold, he paused to stomp his boots so as not to drag any clinging dirt indoors. It was a habit pounded into him as a youth by an eastern-raised mother who, upon moving to the dusty prairie, discovered a seemingly endless need to clean. He could almost hear her reminding him, "Don't you track dirt into my house, young man, or I'll skin you alive." He grinned to himself and shook his head. Memories come back at the strangest times.

He waved away a persistent fly from in front of his face as the tattered screen door banged behind them. He wondered how long it had been since someone had made repairs. The house showed how quickly the harsh, dry desert could exact its toll. He followed dutifully behind as she led him to the stairway straight back.

She took firm hold of the carved newel post, and, then, lifting her skirts so as not to catch the toe of her pointed shoes in the hem of her dress, Mrs. Dunham led the way to an empty room on the second floor.

"Any chance for a bath?" he asked, brushing more trail dust from his vest.

"Just you let me know when you're ready, and I'll put a kettle on to boil. Five cents for the bath, two more if you want that fancy perfumed soap from back east. Tub's at the end of the downstairs hall in the back."

"Old-fashioned soap will suit me just fine," he chuckled.

She pushed open the door to his room, then moved aside

and motioned him in. A single iron bed, flimsy washstand, small basin and ewer, Chatham-square mirror on the wall, and a slat-backed chair constituted the room's major furnishings. A narrow, lace-curtained window looked out on the street below, giving him a good view back toward town. A light breeze wafted the curtains through the half-open window.

"I'll have the stable boy fetch your horse and bed him down, if you'd like," she said as she stepped back into the hall.

"That would be nice, thank you," he answered. "Ask him to feed and curry him. Tell him I'll be by in the morning to settle up."

"I'm sure that'll be fine," she called back, closing the door behind her as she left.

He looked around the room, then decided he'd wait until morning for that bath. For the time being, nothing appealed like the sight of a real bed, with a mattress and clean sheets. It had been three days since he'd slept on anything softer than his blanket spread on the desert ground. And his quarters at Ft. Huachuca were strictly military. No lace curtains allowed.

The iron frame bed squeaked a rusty-springed protest as he collapsed onto it. He settled back with his hands behind his head. He stared up at the ceiling, his mind momentarily returning to the reason he'd come back to Desert Belle: the possibility that the Bishop brothers had somehow miraculously escaped the terrible explosion that rocked the town, all but destroying the old adobe jail. A brief glance at the crumbled building as he passed on his way into town had suggested that deputy Ben Satterfield's imagination may be as big as his belly. The question didn't remain long on Kelly's mind, however, as he fell sound asleep almost immediately, still fully clothed, boots, trail dust and all.

Kelly had failed to pull the blind at the window and was awakened early by bright sunlight shining directly in his face. Although still groggy from little sleep during his several days on the trail, he struggled to his feet, and—rather than give in to the strong temptation to roll over, face-to-the-wall, and fight the call to rise—shuffled sleepily across the small room to the basin to splash the cool water on his face. His bushy mustache dripped as he groped blindly for a towel to dry on. He smiled as he breathed in the distinctive aroma of freshly-brewed coffee drifting into his room, reminding him that for three days all he'd eaten was bad trail food.

As he eagerly entered the dining room, he was greeted by Mrs. Dunham, who directed him to take a seat at the long, harvest table. She placed a cup in front of him and filled it with fresh brew from a steaming, tin pot she carefully held by two well-scorched pot holders. Across from him sat the only other guest to show up for breakfast: a slim, sandy-haired man in a sack suit and a brocade waistcoat, smelling of bay rum. The man failed to even acknowledge the marshal's arrival, keeping his nose firmly buried in a week-old copy of *Harper's Illustrated* newspaper.

"You're risin' later than I'd have expected," Mrs. Dunham said. "Figured the law for early risers."

"Long trip, Ma'am, and the bed was real welcome."

The exchange between the marshal and Mrs. Dunham got the sandy-haired man's attention and he hastily folded his paper, took one last gulp from the coffee cup in front of him, and, noisily pushing his chair back across the bare wood floor, hurried from the room.

"Mr. Cartright, you've not had your eggs," she called after him. She muttered to herself, "Must have been late for some sorta business." She busily gathered the plate, saucer, cup and tinware from his place and started to carry them from the room.

"What line of work is the gentleman in?" Kelly asked.

"J.D.? Oh, I believe he sells supplies to the mines around the area. Drilling tools, picks, shovels and the like, I suppose. Stays with me a day or two each week," she said, leaning her arm across the back of a chair, one hand on her hip. "And how would you be wantin' your eggs, Marshal?"

"Sunny side up, if you please, Ma'am."

* * *

Ben Satterfield sauntered into the sheriff's office and plopped down on a creaky wooden chair. "Sheriff, I been giving this whole affair a lot of thought, and I ain't convinced the Bishops are really dead."

"Of course they're dead. We got two bodies, ain't we?" the sheriff said, shaking his head at the deputy's disbelief of the evidence.

"Yeah, but it don't sit right with me. There's something missin'." Satterfield leaned forward with his fat forearms on his knees, pushed his hat back on his head, and sighed deeply.

"Well, you can put that nonsense out of your mind. Besides, I've got a job for you to do. I want you to take this envelope out to the Lily. Give it to the foreman, Ortez."

"You know Slaughter ain't gonna take kindly to me wanderin' onto his land. He's made that plain." Satterfield asked as he reached for the sealed envelope. "What is it?"

"The bill for damages done to the saloon by a couple of brawlin' miners back a spell," the sheriff said.

"Okay, Sheriff. I'll head out soon's I get a drink to wet my whistle. That's a hot, dusty ride out to the mine."

"All right, but don't take too long. And, remember, that envelope goes to Ortez himself."

Not wanting to head into the desert without sufficient ammunition, Satterfield grabbed two handfuls of shells from the wooden box on the corner of the desk, stuffed them in his coat pocket, then lumbered out of the sheriff's office. Out back, several men were making mortar to begin rebuilding the part of the jail destroyed in the blast. He shouted to one of the men, laughingly encouraging him to make sure to build a dynamite-proof one this time.

He pushed open the batwing doors of the Shot-to-Hell Saloon and chose a seat at the first empty table he came to.

"What'll it be, Ben?" the bartender asked. Ben's entrance had rescued him from the boredom of an empty saloon and the possibility of nodding off mid-morning before he was obliged to start his clean-up from the night before.

"A shot of that swamp water you keep down below, Billy," Ben quipped.

The bartender snorted, pulled a half empty bottle from a low shelf behind the bar, grabbed a glass from atop the back-bar, and brought them to the table where Ben sat like a bull-frog waiting for a fly.

"Anything else?" Billy joined the deputy, leaning forward with his elbows on the table, chin cupped in his hands.

"Yeah, since you ask. What've you heard about the jail explosion?" Satterfield leaned back, scratching at the three-day-old stubble on his face.

"What do you mean?" Billy asked.

"You know, talk. That idle chatter that flits around a saloon at night."

"You got to be more specific, Ben. Cowboys talk a lot of garbage, and that's all most of it is, too."

"Okay, I'll spell it out for you. Has anyone suggested it might not have been the Bishops that got blowed to kingdom come?"

"Only thing I've heard is that it seemed strange the gang used so much dynamite, and that they couldn't be too damned bright. Why do you ask?"

"Well, Billy, I ain't totally convinced it *was* the Bishop brothers at all," Ben said, downing the entire contents of his glass at once.

"Then who was it?" Billy asked, surprised by such a revelation.

"Don't know, but I aim to find out. Thanks for the drink," he said. He stood up from the chair, then shuffled off to collect his horse from the stable and get on with his assignment before Potter found him still in town.

"Where you headed, Ben?" the bartender called after him.

"Out to the Lily. Sheriff wants me to give Henry Ortez the bill for damage to this place after some disturbance a couple of miners caused." Satterfield scratched his head as he continued, barely above a mumble, "Must have slept through that one, though. I can't recall the occasion."

"The memory's always the first to go. The sheriff must have put the fear of God in them boys, though. They ain't been back since he hauled them away."

He saddled his horse at the corral in back of the livery, shoved his carbine in the scabbard, and mounted the old bay mare that had been his companion for ten years. He glanced over at the demolished jail as he passed by it on his way out of town. He shook his head.

It still didn't add up.

Chapter Six

After breakfast, the marshal returned to his sleeping room to gather those essentials lawmen need when venturing onto the streets of any of the mining towns near the San Pedro. He pinned the worn silver badge to his collarless, blue-striped cotton shirt, only to cover it as he slipped into his black vest; retrieved the black leather holster that hung from the bedpost and strapped on the Richards converted, walnut-handled Colt .44. He finger combed back his hair, and placed the cavalry style Stetson on his head. He glanced in the small mirror and ran his hand across his bushy mustache just to assure there were no visible remains from breakfast lingering. The last thing he did as he left the room was reach for his Winchester .44 carbine.

Kelly set out straight-away to look up Sheriff Potter and get his report on the explosion.

The jail, or what was left of it, sat slightly back off the street. Kelly took a short-cut through an alley that would take him down the hill to the low bluff overlooking a creekbed that meandered from the mountains to the San Pedro, and at one point snaked crookedly to within a few feet of the rear of the jail. Though the creek was dry most of the year, when the rains came to the mountains the dry creek turned into a confluent.

He was curious to see for himself how the gang gained

34

access to the jail and how they made their escape. As he came to the clear area behind where the cellblock part of the jail had once stood, it was more than obvious that one hell of a blast had taken place. He didn't see how anyone could have lived through it.

He watched for a minute as workmen piled the debris into mounds of reusable and nonreusable materials. The reusable pile was small. Even the hand-hewn beams that had supported the plank ceiling had splintered in the center from the upward force of the explosion. Those massive beams had then fallen in on the two prisoners and, along with the collapse of the walls, served to seal their doom—had they not already been rent stem to stern by the blast itself. As he glanced about, something didn't seem quite right about what he surveyed.

As he studied the scene, his mind was busy reconstructing the possible chain of events. The first thing out of place was the way the blast had splintered those beams, particularly the heavy timber that served as the center beam. And the way the thick adobe walls had buckled outward. It appeared to him that the explosion had come from inside the cellblock, not outside as would have been the case had the gang tried to secure the release of their leaders by blasting a hole in the back wall. Perhaps Ben Satterfield's concerns were justified. But, he needed to talk to Satterfield himself.

A second concern he had was the lack of a sufficiently clear area behind the jail for a bunch of riders to gather unseen, set a charge, then pull back a safe distance to avoid being blown up themselves. After the explosion, they would need quick access to bring the horses up for the freed prisoners, and an easy, quick escape route.

Over the years, the sudden rushing waters of the creek during the rainy season had cut deeply into the sandstone rise on which the jail sat, leaving a substantial drop-off less than a dozen feet from the back of the jail, making escape in that direction almost impossible. Unless, of course, the Bishop gang was, as had been speculated by many, made up of bumbling fools. Kelly was not quick to accept this theory.

Rounding the corner to the front of the building, he arrived at the front door just as Sheriff Potter was coming out, lighting a cigar.

"Sheriff, glad I caught you before you left. I wanted to talk about the Bishops' fate."

"Well, Marshal, didn't you get my telegram? The Bishops got themselves sent to Hell. Sorry you made the ride for nothing," Potter said, nervously.

"Yes, I got your message, but my natural curiosity got the better of me and I had to see for myself. I'm sure you understand."

"I reckon I do at that. Sorry there wasn't enough left of their bodies to let you get a last look. Guess since you were the one to bring 'em in, you'd have liked to have had a look see."

"Not necessarily, but I am some surprised at the curious way the explosion seems to have taken place. You *are* sure it was the Bishops themselves that were the victims? Couldn't have been somebody else?"

"Are you sayin' you don't believe my explanation, Marshal?" His face flushed and his eyes narrowed at the veiled suggestion of incompetence.

"Oh, no offense, Sheriff, I'll gladly take your word for it. I just have this peculiar need to ask questions, that's all. By the way, is your deputy around?"

"Ben? Why, no. I sent him out to the Gilded Lily mine. Why'd you want to see him? Wasn't him fillin' your head with groundless suspicions, was it?"

"No, nothin' like that. Knew him from a meetin' we had years back. Thought I'd say hello," the marshal lied. But Kelly's easy manner seemed to have put the sheriff at ease. Being confrontational wasn't the young marshal's way to get things done, unless, of course, bullets were involved.

"Oh. You goin' back right away?"

"I may as well stick around for a spell. Nothin's doing elsewhere that needs special attention for the time being. Besides, I'm in no particular hurry to bed down in that rocky desert. Reckon I'll see you around, Sheriff." Kelly touched the brim of his hat in a casual salute and started off in the direction of the saloon nearest the jail, leaving the now curious sheriff looking after him with a frown and scratching his head.

He wasn't satisfied with the sheriff's explanation. Sheriff Potter seemed too defensive, like a man with something to hide. This made the marshal all the more anxious to talk to Satterfield and get his views. But, since the deputy was away, Kelly thought it a good idea to see what he might gather from the best informed people there were: Bartenders.

A heavily-loaded, flat-bed dray pulled by a pair of Belgian horses rattled along in front of him as he crossed the dusty street.

Climbing the two steps to the saloon, he couldn't help noticing the general disrepair of the building. Unusual, he thought, as most successful purveyors of spirits and entertainment keep their establishments painted regularly, and generally well cared for. As he pushed open the door, his nostrils were filled with the aroma of stale smoke, spilled beer, and rotgut whiskey from the night before. It took his eyes a moment to adjust to the dingy darkness of the narrow, near–windowless room.

"Mornin', Marshal. Saw you talkin' to the sheriff. Wondered when you'd be over," the bartender said as he busied himself dragging upside-down chairs off table tops, setting each upright in its proper spot after mopping the floor in preparation for the day's trade. The stout, balding man, with a pot belly earned from too often sampling the products of his trade, stopped work long enough to acknowledge the marshal's arrival.

"What made you think I'd be coming here?" Kelly asked. He walked to the bar, placing the toe of his boot on the brass rail.

"Hunch. Ben Satterfield's been goin' around sayin' he wasn't real sure it was them Bishop boys what got themselves blowed up in the jail. He and the sheriff seem a bit at odds over that theory. What better place than a saloon to check out rumors." With a damp rag he made a half-hearted swipe at a spill he'd missed before.

"Ben ever mention his notion to you?"

"Well, yeah, he was in earlier. We jawed a bit." The bar-tender dropped his towel on a table, then shifted his weight to lean stiff-armed on the back of a chair.

"And what do you think?"

"I've knowed ol' Ben for several years and I never knowed him to go off half-cocked on a hunch." The bartender mo-tioned the marshal to a table near the back, then went to the bar and returned with a bottle and two glasses. "Drink?"

"No, thanks. It's just a bit early in my day. You still didn't say what your thoughts were on the matter," the marshal said. He scooted a chair across the rough floor with his boot and eased onto the edge of it as the bartender settled in across the table from him and began to pour himself a drink. Kelly leaned over to look the man straight in the eye. "Do *you* think the two dead men are the Bishop brothers?"

The bartender began tapping nervously on the table with his fingers. "I-I ain't sure. There has been talk among some of the rougher elements that perhaps—and I say perhaps—them two was someone else. But, that was only hearsay. I don't know nuthin'!" His voice had become nearly a whisper as he leaned over to Kelly so as not to be overheard, though they were completely alone as far as the marshal could tell. If anyone else was around, they had to be hiding.

Something different from what he'd been led to believe by the sheriff seemed to be taking shape. If the Bishops weren't the ones who died in the explosion, then somebody surely had gone to a lot of trouble to make it look that way. Satterfield's doubts, if true, meant Kelly was now involved with a murder, for someone had surely died that night. It also meant Ord and Hale Bishop might still be roaming free.

"If you're suggesting that the Bishops aren't dead, then who might those two corpses have been?"

"I don't know. Look, it's probably just loose talk from some of the toughs that sometimes come across from Tombstone or down from Fairbank. I got no names for you. Wouldn't give you one anyhow."

"Afraid?"

"You can bet on it, Marshal. It don't pay to go mouthin' folks' names to the law hereabouts."

"Okay, I get your drift." Kelly got up to leave, then turned back to the man who had just gulped a half glass whiskey. "If you *were* to get a name, I'd be real forgetful about where it came from, and there might be a small reward if it happened to put me on the right trail. Let me know if you change your mind."

He slapped the bar with the flat of his hand as he passed. The sharp sound startled the perspiring bartender out of his thoughts. Only the sound of Kelly's own boots on the wooden plank floor followed him to the door, echoing off the pine walls and high, tin ceiling of the dusky room.

After Kelly left, the bartender nervously poured himself another, spilling half of it before the glass touched his lips. He walked to the front window to watch the marshal step into the street—his face lined with fear and apprehension as Kelly disappeared into a crowd of milling people busying themselves with the day's commerce. The bartender's thoughts were on something other than selling watered-down whiskey to parched miners.

From the alley across the street, a lone figure stepped back into the shadows when the marshal came through the swinging batwings of the Shot-to-Hell Saloon. As Kelly walked out of view, a hand fell to the grips of a Remington .44 and eased it from its low-slung holster. The owner of that weapon then half-cocked the pistol, and rolled the cylinder through once to confirm its readiness.

It slid easily back into its oiled holster with a practiced half roll.

Chapter Seven

Kelly strolled along the uneven boardwalk that ran in front of the jail, poking his head in business after business in hopes of finding someone who had seen or heard anything unusual the night the Bishop gang supposedly tried to free their leaders. Nobody heard anything, nobody saw anything. A town doesn't just turn to stone at night, he thought. There had to be someone who closed up shop late, or a miner or cowboy sleeping off one too many whiskeys in a lonely doorway, who saw something but didn't realize its importance at the time. He shook his head. He'd just have to keep looking.

At dinner that evening, Mrs. Dunham was her usual cheerful self, hurrying back and forth between the kitchen and the dining room carrying bowls of food like a bee gathering pollen. Mr. Cartright, the salesman, and a young man and his new bride from Santa Fe, were the only other guests that evening. That was the perfect number of people for Mrs. Dunham to handle easily. It afforded her time to lavish special attention on the newlyweds. Kelly was seated at the end of the table with Mr. Cartright to his left.

"Mr. Cartright, I reckon you heard about the explosion that brought the jail down," the marshal said, the first to break the silence. Cartright had made it clear by his hurried exit the previous morning that he wasn't keen on exchanging pleasantries, but Kelly *was* interested in learning more about the man in the sack suit.

"I suppose I heard something about it," Cartright answered curtly without looking up from his plate. "Reckon most have."

"Looks as if it might have taken a powerful lot of dynamite to do that much damage to a building constructed specially to keep such a thing from happening. Wouldn't you say?"

"Can't say I gave it much thought," Cartright answered as he busied himself mopping up brown gravy with a hunk of fresh baked bread.

"I was wonderin' if you ever sell dynamite to the mines hereabouts." Kelly held his cup with both hands, elbows on the table, intent on watching Cartright's every expression.

"I do, along with a great deal of other supplies and various small equipment." Cartright spoke with his head down, concentrating on his food, showing no concern for the marshal's questions. He prepared to drown another hunk of meat under a spoonful of thick gravy.

"So, you'd be a person who could easily enough lay his hands on some sizable amounts of the stuff. Is that a fair assumption?"

"If I was a mind to. Jus' what're you tryin' to say, Marshal? You hinting that I might have had a hand in what happened?" Cartright bristled at Kelly's thinly veiled suggestion. His hands clenched tightly on the knife and fork he held. His eyes narrowed as, for the first time, he looked the marshal straight in the eye. Kelly had finally succeeded in gaining his full attention.

"No, nothing like that." Kelly sat back easily, wiping his mustache with his napkin. "I was just speculatin' on where a body could come by enough explosives to get the job done without raising suspicion as to its possible use. Assuming it didn't come from one of the mines, a person would have to buy it from somewhere nearby, wouldn't he? Thought you might know where."

Apparently satisfied that he wasn't actually being accused of anything, Cartright relaxed a bit and returned to eating. "If they had a mind to, and could come up with a little something extra for the pot, I suspect most anyone could purchase dynamite from the company store." Cartright said casually.

"But don't you think if some rough lookin' characters like the Bishop gang were to ride in here an' try to buy that much dynamite someone would have the good sense to report it to the sheriff?" Kelly leaned forward again with his elbows on the table.

"As I said before, don't know as I give it much thought." Cartright slurped from his cup, then drew a bunched-up napkin across his mouth. He reached across the table and helped himself to more bread. He had reverted totally to his previously detached demeanor. As far as he was concerned, the conversation was concluded.

The marshal had noted Cartright's discomfort at being questioned. He was certain the man knew more than he was telling, but getting him to reveal what he knew wouldn't be easy. He decided to push a bit farther. "Suppose you were asked to sell a large amount of the stuff to strangers, would you sell it to them?"

"No sir, I wouldn't. Company policy. Couldn't anyway. I can sell only to mine operators, company stores, the army, or to a government agency. Everything's done by purchase order. No money changes hands, and I'm bound to keep a strict inventory of those articles I carry with me," Cartright frowned, shaking his fork in Kelly's direction. "I also don't keep dynamite lyin' around in the natural course of business. I been with Southwestern Mining Equipment for seven years and I aim to stay many more."

Kelly decided to accept that the man was nothing more than what he appeared—for the time being anyway. His query had netted him nothing new to go on, so he decided to redirect his attention to the handsome, medium-rare steak growing cold on the plate before him. Juice oozed as his knife sliced cleanly through the pink meat.

As he ate, he glanced up to notice the couple seated to his right. The young man, not much more than a boy, had interrupted his own meal to listen intently to the exchange between Cartright and the marshal. He'd said nothing, but his eyes had followed the conversation as it went back and forth. Kelly smiled at the two of them, nodded, and went back to polishing off the steak.

"I hope everything was to your liking, folks," Mrs. Dunham said as she came bustling back into the room, preparing to relieve the table of empty stoneware bowls and mismatched china dishes. "More coffee, anyone?"

Mr. Cartright grumbled something indiscernible which Mrs. Dunham took for a "no", so she passed him by to offer the contents of the steaming pot to the young woman.

"If it wouldn't be too much trouble, Mrs. Dunham, I'd really prefer tea," she asked. A fair-skinned young woman with mousy brown hair gathered neatly on top of her head, small of frame and features, she seemed almost too delicate to be asked to try surviving the harsh, dangerous life of the desert.

"Deary, I'd love to oblige, but I haven't laid eyes on the real thing for over three years, and what goes for tea around here ain't fit for human consumption. Even cowboys won't touch the stuff, and they're known to imbibe almost anything. I'm real sorry."

"That's all right, I understand. It's just that back east where I came from, we drank tea at almost every meal. I've grown rather used to it." She folded her hands in her lap with a weak smile.

Kelly held his cup in the air as Mrs. Dunham poured the strong brew into it. Cartright scooted his chair back from the table and slipped out of the room without further conversation.

"You two on your honeymoon?" the marshal asked.

"No, sir. Didn't have money for a honeymoon," the young man said. He looked at his wife, who dropped her eyes demurely. "I'm to start my new job next week. That's why we came here from Santa Fe. That's where we got hitched. My name's Carl Sutter, and this here's my wife, Elizabeth."

"Pleased to meet you folks. What's your line of work, Carl?"

"Mining engineer. Just graduated from the School of Mines, and I got a job right off. Out at the Gilded Lily, just west of here. You know where that is, Marshal?"

"Not exactly, but I've heard the name plenty. Sounds like a fine start to your marriage. Good luck to you both," he said, lifting his cup in a salute to the couple. He then gulped the last of his coffee, swiped at his bushy mustache with his napkin, and pushed back to leave the table. The well-worn floor creaked as he stood to go.

"Sir, please excuse my bad manners, but I couldn't help hearing what you and the gentleman were discussing and I got my own theory about what might have occurred that night, if you're interested in hearing me out," Carl said, half raising from his chair.

"Carl, the marshal doesn't have time for any of your theories. Let him be," the girl said in a loud whisper. She put her hand on her husband's arm as if he needed holding in place.

"I'll hear you out, son. What's on your mind?" The marshal sat back down, and crossed his arms in front of him.

"You'll have to excuse my wife, Marshal, she doesn't think I'm old enough to have much in the way of ideas when it comes to things other than engineering."

Kelly smiled and nodded knowingly as the girl blushed, embarrassed by her husband's words.

"Well, anyway, I looked over the site of the explosion when we come to town, and it struck me right off—"

Kelly's curiosity was piqued. "What struck you, son?"

"The way the walls were blown out. That explosion for sure came from the inside, not the outside like folks was sayin'."

"I figured the same. Anything else?"

"See, he knew all along. Your theory isn't anything new, Carl," Elizabeth broke in with I-told-you-so satisfaction.

"Hush. I'm not through, yet," he said with a hurt scowl.

"Go on, son, what else is on your mind?"

"Well, in school we studied blast patterns for all sorts of explosions. I'm of the considerable opinion that it wasn't dynamite at all. Far too much heat expended."

"Not dynamite? What then?"

"Nitro!" Carl said with authority, and a sideways nod to his wife.

Nitroglycerin. Kelly hadn't thought of that. It's a much trickier substance to handle, but takes far less to make a bigger explosion. It would also be easier to sneak into town unnoticed, though by no means was it something sensibly transported in the middle of the night by desperate men on horseback in a hurry to free their leaders from jail. This new line of reasoning lent credence to Deputy Satterfield's contention that all was not as it seemed. Maybe the young engineer was on to something after all. Whether or not nitro was accessible and commonly used in the area might make an interesting question to ask someone out at the Gilded Lily.

It made for a good excuse to take a ride.

Chapter Eight

Deputy Satterfield swayed back and forth astride the old bay mare picking its way through the steamy desert. He continually mopped the dusty sweat from his face, fanning himself with his crumpled hat, and often drawing great gulps from his canteen. He considered this trip a waste of time. The sheriff could have given the bill for damages to King Slaughter the next time he was in town or even sent it out with one of the many miners from the Lily who invaded Desert Belle every weekend. In fact, it was so obviously a ploy to get him out of town, Satterfield seriously considered disobeying his orders and returning to Desert Belle. *It must have been the fuss I been makin' about them Bishops not really bein' dead*, he thought. *I wonder why the sheriff's so dead set against my thoughts on the matter?*

He began to feel a strange uneasiness. Something in the air said things weren't as they should be. The usual sounds of birds were distinctly absent. He glanced around for some reason for his feelings, signs of a roving band of Apaches, a brush fire or a coming storm, anything. But he saw nothing. Uneasily, he continued on, but now fear rode with him.

The shadows were growing long as dusk approached. Rippling waves of heat hung over the green-gray landscape like ghostly flames. Pooder and Blue sat hunched down behind a rocky incline mopping perspiration from their foreheads. Soon, it would be time to execute Pooder's plan.

"This better work, Pooder," Blue admonished his partner.

"Or what?" Pooder shot back.

"Or you're on your own. I didn't have nothin' to do with you shootin' that man. I'll be forced to tell them outlaws just that, too, if this fool plan of yours gets us nabbed."

"You'd go yellow on a friend? Leave me to face that gang alone? Some partner I picked to ride with," Pooder grumbled.

"Well, I didn't tell you to plug that fella, did I?"

"He didn't give me no choice, now did he? He was goin' to plug me first and then you. I had to do it or we'd both be dead by now. I saved your life and this is how you repay me?" Pooder stood up disgustedly, kicked at some dirt and then half-stumbled, half-slid down the incline back to where his horse was tied to the branches of a mesquite bush.

"I—well, I reckon I didn't think none on that part of it. I'm sorry, Pooder," Blue said, scampering down the hill right on Pooder's heels. "I guess I'm with you."

"Good. Now, let's get some food in our bellies. I'm so hungry I'd give my left arm for just one Johnnycake."

The two used all the cover they could find in making their way to the livery stable at the edge of Charleston. They tied their horses to some trees well out of sight of the street that ran in front of Goodman's Livery. The night was dark as pitch as they entered through the back door. Inside, Pooder cupped his hands to his mouth and called out.

"Hello. Anyone here?"

"Up front. What can I do for you?" came a raspy voice.

They made their way to a place near the stalls in front where an old man sat on a wooden keg, rolling a quirly.

"Good evenin', sir," Pooder said. "Me and my friend have come about the job."

"I'm only lookin' for one. Can't use the two of you," the old man said. He squinted in the direction of where the boys stood. "Come over here, in the light, so I can see you better."

Pooder and Blue did as they were told.

"Say, ain't you the two that shot that no-good Johanson? I

heard you lit outta town. What in tarnation are you doin' back?"

"We-we're a mite hungry, an' when we, uh, saw that sign of yours sayin' you was needin' help. Well, we figured you might stake us to a meal if we was to muck out the stables for you," Pooder said.

The old man rubbed his chin and squinted his eyes. "Hmmm," he thought aloud. "I never did cotton to that gun-totin' loudmouth, anyway. Can't say he didn't need killin'. Reckon I could rustle up some grub for a little work at that. Mind you, I can't be watchin' every minute of the day to make sure someone don't see you workin' in here. Come mornin' next, you best be hightailin' it outta here. If that Bishop bunch finds you here, there'll be hell to pay."

"Them was our plans exactly," Blue said with a pleased grin, as they set to work.

The three members of the Bishop gang were intent on spending the evening in the Border Saloon. The usually noisy barroom fell deadly quiet as they entered. No one was eager to get on the mean side of any of these hardcases. It usually meant someone ended up dead. Longevity was on the side of the cautious.

They picked a table where they could watch whoever entered. Blackwater Bill pushed a chair back, then slid into it with hands free to go for his revolver if necessary.

"You still aimin' to go after those that gunned down Johanson?" Abel Short asked.

"Hell, yes, we're goin' after them two," Abel Barton said through gritted teeth, as he slammed his fist down hard on the table. "We can't let no one get away with killin' one of our own."

"But what if the boss comes and we're out chasin' two stupid kids? They told us to join up here and stay put till they come," Blackwater Bill offered.

"You let me worry about the Bishops. I ain't let you boys down yet, have I?" Big Al said, after hastily downing two more shots of whiskey. He made a face at the bitter taste, then quickly poured another.

"That fool Johanson never had a lick of sense. They shouldn't oughta picked him for this job," Abel spoke up.

"They done it because he was a good man with explosives," Big Al said.

"Hell, any damned fool can light a fuse on a bundle of dynamite and run like hell," Blackwater Bill said.

"We ain't talkin' dynamite, here. Nitro. That's what Ord's got planned for this job, same as we used to blow that flimsy jail over in Desert Belle. Now we got only one other knows anything about nitro, an' I can't say yet as how I fully trust that Yankee peddler. I know I ain't touchin' that stuff!" Big Al hammered the table with his glass. "The fool shoulda listened when I told him to stay out of trouble."

"You know how he was. Never had a mind to take heed of nothin'. He damned well rode his own horse," Abel said.

"He sure enough rode his last one this time," Blackwater Bill mumbled through the whiskey, which was beginning to take its toll.

As they continued to toss back one shot after another, their tirade got louder and louder. Suddenly, in a fit of rage over thinking he was being stared at by a young miner, Blackwater Bill jumped up from the table and challenged the surprised young man to draw or get out. The wide-eyed young miner's first instinct was to apologize, but, instead, he found himself suddenly in the grip of his own youthful pride. Perhaps it was the fear of looking like a coward to his fellow miners that made him accept Bill's challenge.

The young miner eased out of his chair, his hand at the ready, but he never had a chance against the lightning draw of Blackwater Bill's blazing .44. In the span of less than thirty seconds, what had started as an innocent curiosity over what was going on at the table where the three gunslingers sat turned into a cold-blooded killing.

The three went back to their boisterous drinking as the youth lay dying, his life's blood soaking into the broad cracks of the worn floor less than ten feet away.

The bartender sent for the constable, who chose to remain in his office. He wasn't going to walk into that bar with three known killers just waiting for an excuse to add a lawman to the night's death count. If he didn't go, he'd still be alive in the morning. The town needed a live constable, not a dead one. He reasoned that nobody ever expected him to go up against real gunmen.

About one o'clock in the morning the drunken trio wandered back to the livery stable to spend the night, though they hadn't told the liveryman of their intentions.

Abel was the first to the door. He yanked it open, nearly losing his balance, then stumbled inside, coming face-to-face with a startled Blue LeBeau. Three feet away, Pooder was loading manure into a wheelbarrow. He looked up in shock to see the three hardcases come bursting in.

"Well, well, look at what we have here; a couple of hard workin' manure movers," Abel Short laughed. Big Al Barton wasn't laughing as his eyes studied the two boys. He sobered quickly.

"You know, boys, it looks like we just happened onto the two that gunned down Johanson. Look that way to you, Bill?" Barton said.

"By damn if it don't. They sure fit the description that fella in the bar give us. Oughta save us a dusty ride. What'll we do with them, Big Al?"

"Reckon we'll keep them with us till Ord and Hale get here. They may want to be in on the hangin'. Comin' up with these two might just take some of the heat off us."

"Fair enough. When are they gettin' here?" Blackwater Bill asked.

"Tomorrow. Soon as they find out about that gold shipment from the Lily," Big Al said. He pulled a coiled-up rope from a wooden peg on the wall and tossed it to Abel Short. "Tie these two up good an' proper. Don't want them gettin' any notion in their heads of leavin' before the necktie party."

Abel Short gleefully began his task of tying the two frightened boys back to back, seated against the upright beam at the end of one of the stalls. First, he tied their hands in back of them, then wrapped the rope completely around their bodies, securing them firmly to the post. When he was finished, he looked at Pooder and said, "Heard you boys left town. You shoulda stayed gone."

The three outlaws were sawing logs in short order, mostly as a result of all the whiskey they'd consumed. Hearing their loud snoring coming from the back of the stable, Pooder whispered to Blue.

"Blue, you awake?"

"Of course I'm awake. How the hell do you expect me to sleep all trussed up?"

"You still got that pig sticker with you?"

"Yeah, it's in my boot, but I don't think I can reach it."

"Well, you best be tryin'. If you don't get that knife and cut us loose, come mornin' we're gonna be swinging like ham in a smokehouse."

"I'm tryin'!" Blue struggled and twisted with all his might. He worked the ropes until his wrists began to bleed, but to no avail. He could not reach the hilt of that knife stuck down in his badly scuffed brogan. He drew his leg back under him in a effort to get his hands on the heel and maybe pull the brogan off. Then the knife should fall free. Still no luck.

"See if you can scoot your leg around the post far enough that I can get my leg on top of your boot, then you pull. Maybe it'll come off," Pooder whispered.

"It won't come off. I need to find a way to get to the laces," Blue cried. He tried as hard as he could. He struggled and stretched for all he was worth, until his legs began to cramp so bad he thought he'd scream. He straightened his leg long enough for the pain to subside, then he tried again. And again. To no avail. There was absolutely no way Blue could get his leg around far enough to let Pooder help. Hours passed, and, exhausted from their efforts, the two boys finally slumped forward, wrists bloody and bodies aching, resigned to whatever lay before them.

A restless sleep overtook them both.

Chapter Nine

Noon the next day found Pooder and Blue still hitched securely to the post in the livery stable. They hadn't seen the three outlaws since being trussed up the night before. They hadn't seen the stable owner, either.

"I wish they'd just come and do whatever they're gonna do to us, Blue," Pooder said. "I've got to pee so bad my eyes are turning yellow."

"Me too. Wish you hadn't brought it up. Now it'll be worse."

"Why's that?" Pooder asked.

" 'Cause, if you talk about a thing and you can't do nothin' about it, it gets worse. Like an itch. You ever try to ignore an itch? It just gets worse if you think about it."

"I don't have an itch, I have to pee!"

"Then cross your legs. That'll help." Blue squirmed to try finding a more comfortable position, but the ropes just cut deeper into his wrists. "Damn! Why don't they just kill us and get it over with?"

"I think I'd rather pee in my pants than get killed," Pooder grumbled.

They heard voices approaching from the back of the stable. It was Big Al Barton and three other voices they'd not heard before. Pooder strained to hear what was being said.

"Didn't expect you until later today. When's the action start?" Big Al asked.

"Four days, that's when they plan to ship a million in gold. J.D. here says it promises to be the biggest haul we've ever laid eyes on," another man said.

"Whooee! That'll be somethin' to see." Big Al's unmistakable voice rang with excitement over the prospect of seeing a fortune in gold.

"How many guards you figure they'll post, Ord?" Abel Short cut in.

"At least ten, I figure. The six of us can take them, though."

"Got some bad news, Ord," Blackwater Bill piped up. "There'll only be the five of us, unless we pick up some help from Tombstone."

"Five? What happened to Johanson? Didn't he get here like I told him?"

"Yeah, sure, Ord, he got here. But some dumb farmer kid faced him down in the street, an' got the best of ol' Johanson," Big Al answered. "He's deader than a rock!"

"Damn the luck! Now we only got J.D. to handle the nitro. Damn! Where is this kid?"

"We got him, Ord. We got him tied up like a Christmas goose. Got his partner, too. We was waitin' for you and Hale to get here to hang them both." Big Al led the others into the back room where the boys were being held.

"Hell, Big Al, you shoulda just plugged them. We ain't got time to mess with stringin' them up. We got to get our plans set to take that Lily shipment. And we got a lot of ridin' to do."

"Well, what'll we do with them kids?"

"Shoot them! Right after we get some breakfast and pick up a few supplies, we'll plug them where they sit. If we do it now, someone'll hear the shots. I don't aim to ride until I've filled my belly. Now, let's find us some grub."

The five men strode past Pooder and Blue as they left through the front doors of the livery. The man in the lead glanced down at the boys as he went. Pooder shuddered at the look in the man's cruel, gray eyes.

Pooder waited until he was sure they were gone before he spoke. "Did you hear what they called them two ugly ones? Ord and Hale! Them's the Bishop brothers."

"I thought they got blowed up over in Desert Belle," Blue whispered back.

"Unless we was just lookin' at a couple of ghosts, they didn't. Don't know who the fancy one was, though, the one they called J.D."

"What're we gonna do, now? Soon's they get back, we're dead." Blue wriggled at his bonds in some faint hope they'd miraculously loosened during the night. They hadn't.

Just then, Pooder thought he heard a sound coming from the back near the last stalls. "What was that?" he said.

"What was what?" Blue answered.

"That sound. Like a moan. Someone's back there." He heard it again. He called out, "Who's there?"

They both heard what sounded like something being dragged across the dirt floor, coming toward them. It was the old man. He was bleeding badly from a gash on his forehead, and trying to crawl toward them, pulling himself along with one arm as the other dangled uselessly. The arm appeared to be broken. Blood streamed down his face, filling his eyes.

As he struggled to get near where the boys were tied, he stopped several feet away, out of reach, gasping for a breath and sweating heavily. The effort to make his way was more than the old man's body could take. He had been kicked and bludgeoned into near unconsciousness. Now, barely able to function, he had to rest. But resting took time, and time was something all three were running out of.

"Old man, over here. Can you see us?" Pooder called out.

"I-I can hear you, can't quite make out wh-where you are, though," he said, fighting to keep from blacking out as his good arm gave out and he slipped face down in the dirt.

"What happened to you, mister?" Pooder asked.

"D-don't know. Some men shook me awake just before dawn, and then began beatin' on me with their pistol butts. D-didn't think they'd ever s-stop," the old man cried.

"We need your help, Sir," Blue said in a low, frightened voice.

"Give m-me a minute t-to rest here."

"We ain't got a minute, old man," Pooder pleaded. "Them

Bishops are probably on their way now. You're our only chance. They're gonna kill us when they get back here. Please try." His loud whisper squeaked from the panic welling up inside.

The old man raised his head, then began clawing at the hard-packed floor in an attempt to get to the boys. Slowly, he edged closer, near enough to touch Blue's boot.

"That's it, mister, my boot. There's a knife in my boot. If you can reach it and cut us loose, we'll be out of here in a flash," Blue said.

The man fumbled to get a grip on the hilt of the knife. He wrapped feeble fingers around the top of the brass hilt that barely showed itself above the top of Blue's right brogan, clawing and tugging to free it from its hiding place. As he nearly had it all the way out, his eyes rolled back in his head, he gasped and fell forward, unconscious. As he passed out, the old man's hand drew spasmodically back toward him. The knife fell free of the boot, but now lay a few inches from where Blue could get a hold of it.

"Damn!" he moaned. "It ain't quite within reach."

"Try dragging it closer with your foot. Maybe then it'll be near enough to grab."

"Maybe," Blue whispered, as he shot his leg out stiffly to hook the handle on his boot heel. "I can reach it, but it's hanging up on the hard-packed dirt, Pooder. What'll we do now?"

Just then, they heard the unmistakable voices of the Bishop gang returning from breakfast at Dolly's Diner, across the street from the livery. The boys' faces fell as they realized their time on earth was limited.

The rickety door at the front of the room where Pooder and Blue were bound burst open, and in walked the five men, laughing and joking. Abel Short looked over at the old man, sprawled on the ground about two feet away from the boys.

"Looks like the old man tried to get them free. That pistol whippin' you gave him done him in, though," he said. "What do you want us to do with them other two, Ord?"

"We got to gather our supplies, Abe. Take them out back into the brush and shoot them. Far enough away so as to not arouse the suspicion of the constable. We'll ride when you get back."

Abel Short bent down and began to untie the rope that had secured the boys to the post. As he did, the rope fell slack and Blue fell forward on the hard dirt floor. Unnoticed, he managed to roll over and scoop up the knife that he had been able to keep from their view with his boot just as the outlaws returned. He tried to hold it so it would be covered by his shirttails.

"All right you two, get your scrawny butts up on your feet," Abel said. The two boys struggled to keep their unsteady balance as they got to their feet. Abel moved back, drew his six-shooter and motioned for them to head for the side door. They did as they were ordered, stumbling toward the door.

Outside, in the brilliant sun, Short shoved the two down the hill into a ravine. "Keep walkin' you two. It'll all be over soon." He laughed and slapped Blue hard on the shoulder. The jolt knocked the knife from Blue's hand, and it fell to the ground with a thud.

"Well, well, what do we have here?" said Short, picking up the old knife to examine it. The six-inch blade glinted in the sunlight. "You fixin' to cut me or something?"

He gave Blue another hard shove, but the loose stones on the rocky slope began to shift, causing Blue to stiffen and pitch backward to keep his balance. He fell back against Able Short who was studying the knife, turning it around and around in his hand, admiring the strange bone handle. Unfortunately for Short, the blade was pointed right at him as Blue's weight drove the knife deep into the outlaw's chest.

The outlaw's gun fell from his hand as he gasped with pain and grabbed at the hilt of the knife, staring with incredulity at the carved bone with the brass hilt erupting from a bright, red stain spreading rapidly over the front of his shirt. His eyes rolled as he tried to call out, but blood from a severed artery was spurting into his lungs, then, bubbling upwards, filling his mouth and windpipe. He heaved forward with a strangled cry, stumbled, fell to the hard ground, and died.

For a moment Blue and Pooder stood staring at the man

whose body shook briefly in the throes of death, then Blue came to his senses as he realized escape was now possible.

"Pooder, back up to me and let me cut you loose," Blue said, squatting down backwards to retrieve the knife from Abel's chest. With some difficulty, twisting the hilt back and forth, he was finally able to free it.

Without hesitation, Pooder stumbled toward Blue. They both stared in disbelief at the dead outlaw as the blade finally cut through the last strand of rope and Pooder was freed. He quickly seized the knife from Blue's hand, and cut his friend's bindings, also. Then, Blue bent over and scooped up Abel's gun from where the outlaw had dropped it. He blew the dirt from the barrel and cylinder. Then, at the same time, he reached down and relieved the dead man of his holster and gun belt.

"He won't be needing them anymore," he said proudly, hefting the six–shooter in the air, then slipping it back into the leather holster he'd buckled around his slim waist. It hung like too much laundry on a line. "Looks like I'll have to cut another notch in the belt." He grinned.

"Well, you may get to use it before long, friend. We ain't free from that bunch, yet. They'll come lookin' for him soon's they start to wonderin' what's takin' him so long. Let's ske-daddle outta here!" Pooder scrambled up the hill, loosing footing on the gravel with each panicked step. He suddenly fell on his belly out of sight behind a small outcropping of mesquite as a wagon rattled down the street some twenty feet away. "Best be prayin' that our mounts are still staked out over there in that arroyo."

"Don't you worry none about that. I been doin' plenty of prayin' ever since I met you," Blue snorted.

They scrambled down the hill toward where they'd left their mounts—Pooder's old gray, and Blue's white-faced mule. Pooder let out a sigh of relief as they found them, right where they'd left them. They mounted quickly and rode hell-bent-for-leather into the scrub brush strewn desert to the south.

Straight for Desert Belle.

Chapter Ten

Deep in thought, Kelly lay staring at the ceiling in his cramped room at the boarding house. He had a bad feeling about the conflict between the sheriff and his deputy, and about whether the Bishops actually were the two corpses found in the rubble. If anyone in town had the answers, no one was talking. At this point, however, he had no reason to doubt either lawman. And that presented a problem. They couldn't both be right.

Suddenly, the silence was broken by the sound of the floor creaking outside his room. The sound stopped at his door. Instinctively, Kelly threw himself off the bed just as the door burst open, the flimsy lock splintered by a mighty kick. Two quick shots rang out. The slugs from a blazing .44 buried themselves in the mattress, blowing ticking and feathers high in the air, where a split-second earlier the marshal had lain.

As he dove for the floor, with one quick, fluid movement he gathered up his Winchester which had been propped against the wall next to the bed within easy reach for just such an occasion. He thumbed back the hammer, fired, then levered another round into the chamber with such quickness that the man standing in the doorway was caught completely off guard. The two shots came in rapid succession, sounding as one long, echoing blast. The tables had been turned on the gunman, who'd hoped to get the drop on the marshal and kill him before he could get to that deadly rifle.

Crack crack—

Marshal Kelly's attacker was thrown back through the open door and slammed against the wall across the hall. He slumped heavily to the floor with a thud; two slugs hardly more than an inch apart had exploded his heart.

Kelly leapt to his feet, crossing the gunsmoke-filled room in two large steps. He burst into the hall, his whole body spinning first left then right, rifle ready should there be an accomplice of the dead man's. Finding no one, he knelt down beside the fallen gunslinger. He recognized the man as one he'd seen from his window the day before in close conversation with the sheriff.

Nearly out of breath, a wide-eyed Mrs. Dunham came rushing up the steps. She stopped suddenly as she reached the top, coming upon the dead gunslinger sprawled in a pool of blood in the middle of the hallway. She gasped, clutching a towel with which she been drying dishes to her chest.

"I-I thought I said n-no gunplay indoors, M-Marshal," she said with a weak frown, looking pale and faint.

"Sorry, Ma'am," the marshal answered, "but this fella didn't give me a chance to explain the house rules."

He stepped over the body, eased past the shaken woman, and headed down the stairs. "I'll send the sheriff over to clean up," he said as he reached the bottom. "Might be a friend of his."

He strode angrily out of the house toward the jail. He shoved open the door and, finding the office empty, just as quickly slammed the door closed. A man passing by stopped.

"You lookin' for the sheriff, Marshal?" he asked.

"Yes. You seen him recently?"

"Sure did, just a few minutes ago. He mounted up and rode out of town. Looked like he was headin' for the Lily with his britches on fire," the man said, turning to point in the direction of the mine. "Say, what was them shots all about?"

"Obliged," Kelly said, ignoring the man's question. He stormed off toward the livery.

If the sheriff had left only minutes earlier, he'd likely also heard the shots. The whole town probably had. The sheriff had to have known what the shooting was all about. His running was a good indication he probably had a hand in it. If not, he still had a lot of explaining to do. And an explanation was what the marshal meant to have as he went straight-away to the livery where his black gelding was boarded.

The trail into the hilly mine country was rugged and treacherous, but easy to track in. The man back in town had given the marshal good information. A rider had recently ridden the same trail. That rider, too, was in a hurry, judging by the signs left in the sandy soil. Kelly pushed the gelding hard in hope of catching the sheriff before he reached the Gilded Lily mine.

Suddenly, the twisting trail brought a surprise: the unmistakable chatter of a sidewinder in a mood to strike. The gelding shied at the sound. Ironically, the rattler, intent on defending its territory, saved Kelly's life.

As the gelding reared, a bullet sang past the marshal's ear. It missed by inches. Before the sound of the muzzle blast had a chance to catch up, Kelly had slipped the saddle and was sprawled on the rocky ground, rifle at the ready. He had slapped the gelding on the neck as he left the saddle to startle the animal into leaving the line of fire.

A second shot rang out. The bullet exploded the ground nearby, spraying him with dirt. Another near miss. He scampered for the relative safety of a clump of thorny mesquite, beneath a small rocky outcropping. Spitting dust and keeping himself as flat to the ground as possible, he tried to get a fix on his attacker. His eyes searched the scrubby chaparral in the general direction from which the shots had come. Then, just when he expected another bullet to be sent his way to keep him pinned down, he heard the hoof beats of a horse making hurried tracks away from him.

Slowly, Kelly eased into the open, taking care to stay low. He saw a small cloud of dust rising, then disappearing into the distance. He couldn't identify the rider before he vanished into the brush, but it was easy to tell he wasn't staying around to complete the job.

Kelly's Irish temper was beginning to boil inside him. He'd not even gotten a glimpse of the shooter, no opportunity to get even one round off. He was dirty, hot, and tired of getting shot at. He was also confused by all that had occurred in the last few hours. Why would his coming to Desert Belle to check out the deaths of the Bishop brothers make him the target of at least two attempts on his life? And why was the sheriff so chummy with the one lying dead in the upstairs hall of the boarding house?

Had whoever tried to drygulch him only intended to scare him away? If so, from what? Was the sheriff involved? If the intent was to kill him, why hadn't the shooter stuck around to finish the job? These questions would go unanswered for the time being as he rode onto the property posted "no trespassing" by order of the Gilded Lily Mine Corporation. He rode with the muzzle of his rifle pointing skyward, the butt plate seated firmly against his thigh, and his finger on the trigger. He wasn't looking for more trouble, but since it had sought him out twice already today, he figured to be ready for whatever lay ahead.

Given the lateness of the day, the marshal knew there was little point in trying to track the shooter. He would just stay on the trail to the mine to find the sheriff.

Kelly was surrounded by twenty thousand acres of flat, sparsely grassed, featureless desert that ringed a sudden, jutting mountain. That mountain coveted the richest vein of gold ore for many miles around. King Slaughter owned it all. But, Slaughter's mining interests were remote and difficult to defend. He had to take precautions.

Well-armed riders patrolled the great expanse of sand, scrub and rocks to keep would-be independents from sinking a shaft anywhere near the Lily and tapping into a vein by sheer luck. The word was out that any prospectors found on his land might not be heard from again. But claim jumpers weren't his only concern. There were other, more deadly adversaries in that part of the country.

Bands of roving Apaches could be seen from time to time, and their potential for mayhem was not to be underestimated. Slaughter had, on occasion, met with some of the Apache chiefs and knew that generally they were more interested in feeding their families than in his mining operation. Yet, Slaughter was no fool, either. In order to get some assurance that his wagons hauling gold bullion and supplies in and out of camp wouldn't be constantly harassed, he made sure there were always a few scrawny longhorns wandering aimlessly through the brush in search of a few snippets of green foliage. The cattle mostly stuck to the dry creekbeds, a likely spot to find small pools of water and any available grass, so they weren't too hard to find. As long as the Indians were guaranteed food when they needed it, they had been content to let Slaughter's wagons pass unmolested. The life-line of his operation was safe as long as the beef held out.

Piedmont Kelly rode the dusty, winding trail uneasily. He couldn't escape the nagging feeling that he was again being lined up in someone's sights, though he'd seen nothing to give him cause for alarm since entering Slaughter's land. However, he'd had that gut twitching sense of impending danger many times before, and each time it had proven correct. He felt the need to keep a particularly keen eye out ahead of him. And the feeling was growing steadily stronger.

He reined the gelding to a halt. The great horse snorted and shook his head, tugging at the reins, then he obediently stood perfectly still. All Kelly could hear was the hot wind whistling through the brittle locoweed beside the trail and the occasional flutter of small birds coming and going from nests in nearby cacti. Then, the breeze from behind carried something new to his senses. It was the distinct aroma of tobacco smoke. A cigar, he thought. He turned in the saddle, but before he could bring the Winchester to bear, he was hit hard from behind. A bullet slammed into him from the back. Then the echoing bark of a gun's discharge followed a split-second later. He was thrown forward onto the neck of the great horse, who started to gallop forward, then turned off the trail after several yards and came to a halt as the reins slipped from the young marshal's hands. Dazed and disoriented, Kelly tried in vain to cling to the horse's neck, and, failing this, he slid from the saddle, crashing hard to the ground. The gelding, trained to stand at the drop of the reins, patiently stood guard by his fallen master.

The marshal lay still, without the gumption to even attempt moving. His brain seemed unable to grasp what had occurred, and why he was suddenly lying in the dirt breathing deeply the musty smell of the ageless desert soil. His head said just get up, get back in the saddle and ride away from whatever it was that caused this ignominious relocation of his body from horse to desert; but his muscles couldn't make the connection. Movement of any kind, for the moment at least, proved impossible.

The heat from the ground burned through his clothing in agonizing waves. He silently prayed for the air to remain still so his scent wouldn't be blown into the nostrils of a starving coyote or catamount slipping silently through the brush. Disjointed thoughts of that nature came and went like the mournful whistle of the trains that snaked across the Kansas plains of his youth. That sound, like his fevered mind now, screamed eerily, then raced off into the distance, giving the ears brief respite, only to return again and again. How he hated the certainty of that whistle's return, as it drifted over the waving grasses amidst the acrid smell of the spark-laden smoke held close to the ground by suffocating heat. He now felt the same heat sucking the life from him, stabbing then retreating, gnawing at his will to fight off the pain. Sleep. That was the answer. A short sleep would free him from whatever had befallen him. He would awake renewed, more able to evaluate his predicament. The light began to fade. Yes, the welcome blackness of sleep. Just a little time away from the stabbing pain.

Chapter Eleven

Kelly regained consciousness only briefly, aware of a searing heat in his shoulder, and a mouthful of dirt. For that short time, he thought he heard cattle bawling, probably a small herd on the move, he thought. Then, once again, blackness overtook him like a great curtain being draped over his whole body, and he drifted away in blessed relief from the pain.

Suddenly, the lanky marshal's eyes blinked open. His body was being jostled relentlessly as he lay flat on his back in the rear of a Studebaker wagon bouncing over a rough road. Stabs of pain came now. At first, all he could make out was the blazing sun blinding him. Groggy and disoriented, he tried to turn his head, to get a fix on what was happening to him. Kelly could only make out that he was in a wagon being driven furiously through the rough, rocky desert by a stout driver slapping the reins and shouting to a two-mule team. But this was no ordinary mule-skinner. The driver was a woman.

She turned in the seat to make sure he was still alive. She was sturdily built, with a slightly turned-down mouth, and deep-set eyes that narrowed to slits to compensate for the searing sun. Thinning, curly, salt and pepper hair half-framed a face that showed the rigors of years of hard work, yet revealed an innate love of life. Strong arms strained the rolled-up sleeves of a plaid work shirt, low-heeled boots peeked out from beneath britches too long and too tight. Her whole body

64

seemed to roll with the rhythm of the wagon like she'd been born to the rig.

As the wagon came to a lumbering, dusty halt, the driver vaulted from the padded seat and commenced shouting orders to several men milling around outside a tent.

"Let's see some help over here, you worthless coyotes! This man's been backshot an' he's hurt bad! Help me get him inside the infirmary! Joe, fetch Doc Jones, and be quick about it!" she shouted.

They all moved at once, like scared rabbits flushed from hiding by a ravenous wolf. Gently, two big men lifted the marshal from the wagon and carried him into a high-walled, canvas-covered structure. They placed him on a cot, then left. The woman came to his side, frowned, and then spoke in a raspy voice that sounded more like an old man than a woman.

"You'll be fine, Mister," she said. "Lost a lot of blood, though, so you'll be down for a spell, I'll bet."

Kelly struggled to talk. His mouth was dry and still full of desert dust. "Could you find some water, please?" he whispered.

"You bet." She stomped across the tent to a table with a barrel sitting on top near the edge. She took a tin cup from a stack of them and put it under the barrel spigot. A minute later, she returned, handed him the cup, and then placed her arm gently behind his neck to lift him just enough to swallow. He drank it down in nearly one gulp. He fell back with a groan, grateful for the water, but incensed at the painful fate that had befallen him.

"Thank you," he said. "For the water, and for bringing me in. Who are you, anyway?"

"Molly McQueen. Most folks just call me Mule Molly," she said, pulling a short stool over to his cot. "Mule skinner extraordinaire!" She tossed her head back with a roar of laughter, slapping her thigh. Her well-lined face seemed to smile from top to bottom.

"Mule Molly? That's a strange name. How'd you come by it?" He grimaced as he spoke. It hurt to talk but he didn't want to drift back into that awful blackness.

"You shouldn't be wastin' your energy askin' such darn fool

questions. But, since you've nowhere to go till the doc gets here, I'll tell you. I used to drive salt wagons up in Utah. Took twenty mules to haul those big wagons. When one of them critters would get balky, I'd just get down off the wagon, walk up to the mule what was givin' me fits and bust him right between the eyes with this," she said proudly holding up a gloved fist. "It worked. I seldom had any bad-acting mules after that."

He wasn't certain, but he thought he saw a slight twinkle in her eye. But then, to look at her, it did seem possible she could whip a mule into shape.

"Hmm. I can remember some fights where I wish you'd been around. How'd you happen on me?"

"Spotted your horse. He was standin' next to you like a sentry. You was off the road about ten, fifteen yards. So, I hoisted you into the wagon and brung you here to the Lily. Got your gelding tied outside, too. I'll see to it he gets fed and watered."

"Thanks. You say we're at the Gilded Lily?" Kelly managed with a voice weakening from pain and loss of blood.

"Yep, that's the place."

"I'm grateful you came along," he said. "How long was I out here?"

"From the looks of you, I'd say all night and half a day."

"You work for this outfit?"

"I reckon I wear several hats here. Mostly drive the supply wagon from Desert Belle to the Gilded Lily three times a week for Mr. Slaughter," she said. "I was on my way back when I saw you comin' close to bein' buzzard bait. Who shot you?"

"I don't know. Never saw a soul before I was hit." He tried to turn to find a more comfortable position, but the pain prevented him moving to any great degree. Molly sensed his extreme discomfort.

"Doc'll be here in a minute," she said, seeing the strain in his eyes from his wound. "We got a full-time doctor here at the Lily. So many of these young fools that come out here to work down in the shafts don't have no idea how dangerous it is. They're all the time gettin' hurt.

Just then the canvas-covered frame door was thrust open and a slight, bent-over man with a white beard and a dirty gray suit shoved his way in. He carried a black valise that rattled when he dropped it onto the table next to the cot.

"I'm Doctor Jones, young man. Let's take a look at you." Kelly winced from the pain as the man carefully half-rolled him over on his side, then turned to Molly and said, "Help me get his vest and shirt off, then we'll roll him over on his stomach. Looks like I'm going to have to get a bullet out of this man's back."

The doctor pulled a bottle of whiskey out of his bag, poured some in the tin cup, then added to it by tapping in some cloudy liquid from a small bottle.

"What's that stuff?" Molly asked.

"Laudanum. It'll help cut some of the pain while I dig around for that piece of lead." He handed the concoction to Kelly, who tasted it, made a prunish face, then gulped the whole cup quickly. He'd seen what men had gone through before when they had bullets dug out without anything for the pain. He'd take his medicine, and be glad for it.

The whiskey and laudanum began to take effect, and Kelly could feel himself drifting off into a foggy haze, not quite asleep, but not fully awake, either. Shadows cast on the canvas walls of the wood-frame tent by the flickering light of the lanterns brought back memories of his childhood when branches outside his window sent the moon's light shimmering about. Sharp stabs of pain brought him to the surface of consciousness, then dropped him back into pits of warm molasses.

Several hours later, Kelly awoke fully to find the sun setting, causing one side of the canvas building to glow warmly. The smell of a tent in the hot sun reminded him of his visits to the Union Cavalry camps back in Nebraska at the end of the war between the states.

He looked around to find himself alone. He pushed himself up on one elbow, but quickly fell back as a rush of pain reminded him of his predicament.

"Well, I see you've decided not to die after all, huh?" the doctor said as he pushed open the door to find Kelly rubbing his injured left shoulder. He was wrapped completely around, from his shoulder nearly to his waist with wide strips of white cloth.

"I guess you'd be the one to know whether I'll live or not, Doc," Kelly said weakly.

"You will. Now that you're awake, I'd like to take a peek at my handiwork." The doctor helped the marshal to a sitting position. Kelly winced as the bandage was pulled away from the wound. "Nasty hole, son, but you'll recover nicely. Lucky the bullet wasn't any closer to the lung or you'd be food for the desert critters by now."

"When can I get out of here and get on the trail of the son of a gun who put this hole in me?"

"I'd take it easy for a couple days. That wound needs to heal up or the stitches might break open and start bleeding again."

"Damn," Kelly muttered. Then, an unpleasant memory came rushing back to him as he breathed in a familiar aroma.

"Well, Doctor, how's the patient doing?" came the voice from the open doorway. In walked Sheriff Potter, filling the tent with blue smoke from a large, expensive cigar. "Marshal, they told me you had a little run-in. I got here as soon as I could."

"I was on my way to find you when someone dry-gulched me. Wouldn't have any idea who that someone might be, would you, Sheriff?" Kelly said.

"Why, how would I know that? I ain't seen any back-shootin' types hanging around lately." He smiled and raised his eyebrows innocently.

"How about that *hombre* that burst into my room and tried to fill me with lead just before I came lookin' for you? By now you know I had to kill him. You sayin' you didn't know him?"

"Sure, I knowed him, but that don't mean I had any notion of his intentions, does it?" The sheriff shifted nervously from one foot to another, thrusting his hands in the pockets of his baggy trousers. "I, uh, I got to be gettin' back to town. You get well fast, you hear? We'll talk when you're back on your feet," he said. He hurried from the tent, mounted his horse, and rode away from the mine as if someone had set his britches on fire.

Kelly had the strange feeling he'd just been talking to the man who bushwhacked him. But, he had no way to prove it, and no idea why. Yet.

"What'd you say to put fire to his heels, Marshal?" Molly said, crossing to stand beside his cot.

"I'm not sure myself, Molly. Something seemed to spook him, though, didn't it?" Kelly was even more sure the sheriff knew more than he was saying, since Molly also picked up on his nervous exit.

"Well, I wouldn't put too much stock in him. He's a strange one," she said, pulling up a stool to sit down. "Anything I can get you?"

"You've done more than your share already, Molly." He smiled. Shyly, she returned it. "Be obliged if you'd keep your ear out for anything you hear about folks who take sport in backshootin'."

She nodded as she took her leave.

Kelly just stared at the wall. Sometimes his thoughts turned to just what the hell he was doing in this business. This was one of those times—a time of introspection.

He could have become whatever he'd wanted. Any type of work without the constant threat of having his head blown off by some fool with enough money to buy a gun would do. The territory seemed to be filling up with deranged, perverted gunmen. Too many like John Wesley Hardin and Bill Longley. Sometimes, they even showed up on both sides of the law.

But, after the self-doubt wanes, one must face his own truth. For Piedmont Kelly that truth was: There was nothing that made him feel as alive as wearing that badge, facing each day without knowing if it could be his last. That heightened sense of one's mortality keeps a man's eye a little sharper, his hearing a little keener, and the sense of self-preservation very alert. For Kelly that was what being a lawman was all about.

What life was all about.

Chapter Twelve

Zeb Pooder and Blue LeBeau were without food or water in a hostile desert. They were lucky to have escaped with their lives from the Bishop gang who, they figured, would be hot on their trail with every intent of shooting on sight the two youths who'd somehow managed to kill two of their outlaw bunch. They would be relentless in their pursuit of the farm boy and his dark-skinned cohort, and bring about their immediate demise.

The two boys found a giant outcropping of boulders, interspersed with mesquite, prickly pear cactus, and white brittlebush, on the south side of a narrow ridge of mountains that lay between Charleston and Desert Belle. It would serve as a safe, if temporary, place to rest, as well as a good lookout point from which to observe their back trail. Without water, they had to be careful not to push too hard or their mounts might give out and leave them afoot, which would amount to certain death.

"We'll set a spell here, Blue," Pooder said. He dismounted and led his horse into a stand of mesquite out of sight of anyone coming up the trail. "Best bring that mule of yours up here, too."

Blue did as he was told, and then climbed up as high as he could to get a better view of the valley below. He shaded his eyes from the relentless glare of the noonday sun, straining to catch sight of any movement that might mean their pursuers were closing in. He strained to see as far as he could, but saw no movement of any kind.

Pooder climbed up beside his friend. "See anything, Blue?"

"No. Not even a coyote. You don't suppose we lost them, do you?" Blue asked hopefully.

"Not a chance. They're on our trail, that's for sure. Seems like I can almost smell 'em, what with their whiskey breath and cigar-smoked clothes," he said, pulling a face. "We'll rest here for a spell, then head down that ridge over yonder. If we keep to the far side, they may not cut our trail before we can get beyond those two hazy peaks and make a run for it. That looks like our chance."

Pooder slid down the shady side of one of the boulders and sat propped up against the base of it, with his arms crossed over his chest. He closed his eyes.

"This ain't no time for a nap, Pooder. There are four armed killers lookin' to shoot us full of holes 'afore we finish growin' up," Blue admonished, knowing full well Pooder could fall asleep on a galloping horse. Pooder ignored him as his head dipped. Blue *knew* he was talking to the wind. He shrugged his shoulders, then commenced to climb to a higher place. Settling atop a broad, flat boulder, he raised a hand to shade his eyes and returned to scanning the horizon for signs of any outlaws.

Two hours passed as Pooder dozed. Blue LeBeau stood his watch with the diligence of an army sentry. But he was growing weary of being the sole source of early warning. It was time the responsibility was shared. Suddenly, as he called to Pooder to wake up, he saw a small cloud of dust rising from the far side of the valley. It couldn't have been the Bishops, he thought. The direction was wrong. But, when you're on the run and scared half to death, the slightest movement makes the hair on the back of your neck stand up.

"Pooder," Blue called out. "Wake up! Somebody's comin'."

Shaken from his sleep by the warning, Pooder hastily climbed the rocks to reach Blue's side. He rubbed his still sleep-filled eyes. "Where? I don't see nothin'," he said.

"Across the valley, over there."

"Them Bishops can't be comin' from over that way. They'd be behind us. Must be somebody else." Pooder started to return to his resting place, stopped, then squinted at the dust rising off in the distance. "Wonder who that somebody could be, though. Maybe it's someone who could give us a hand at gettin' away from that bunch of crazy cutthroats."

They both watched as the dust cloud turned into a rider coming in their general direction. LeBeau looked around just in time to catch a glimpse of a larger dust cloud coming from the direction of Charleston. The direction they'd just come. That would be the Bishops. The boys looked at each other in panic.

"I told you we didn't have time for no naps," Blue gritted his teeth as he spoke angrily. "I'm for gettin' outta here, now."

"Hold on. We don't know who that single rider is, but in about ten minutes he's going to run smack into them Bishops. It might just give us time to slip down to the other side and head for that canyon. Let's sit tight and watch."

Sure enough, after a few minutes, the single rider met up with the four coming from the opposite direction. It looked from where Pooder stood that it was an intentional meeting, not one of chance. Perhaps the Bishop gang had sent a telegram to Desert Belle to another gang member to start riding toward Charleston. That would put the boys in the middle with no escape route. Or, it could also be that the man who was meeting the gang in the middle of the desert had planned to be there.

"Maybe that lone rider's comin' with information about that gold they was talkin' about," Pooder said.

"Could be," Blue answered. "Maybe it means they've got more important things to think about than chasin' the two of us."

"That sure as hell is wishful thinking, Blue. We ain't gonna be that lucky, I'd stake my life on it."

"Then what're we gonna do?"

"Like I said before, we sit back and watch."

* * *

"How come we're leavin' the trail of them murderin' kids, Ord?" Big Al Barton said. He rode alongside Blackwater Bill with Ord and Hale Bishop in the lead. They had abandoned the trail they'd been following for several hours, a trail that would lead them into the hills where they were sure the two boys had gone to hide.

"Don't worry, there's time to tend to them later," Ord said. He turned in his saddle to glance back at Big Al. Big Al was scowling at the thought of losing the trail of the two who'd been responsible for the deaths of two of his friends. "I got no intention of lettin' them two get away with what they done."

Reassured for the moment, Big Al shrugged his shoulders and nodded his acceptance. Blackwater Bill, however, wasn't as easily convinced. He started to continue the questioning when Ord held up his hand at the sight of an oncoming rider. Big Al and Bill both pulled their six-guns. Hale told them to holster their weapons.

"Is that someone you know?" Bill asked Hale.

"Yep. He's bringin' news of the gold. We planned to meet him out here at the Flats."

Nearby, the remains of an abandoned stage coach stop called Saguaro Flats was being reclaimed by the desert. Signs of its demise were all around—corrals broken down, barn burned almost to the ground, the roof of the adobe building where the stage master lived had crumbled into the single room.

"What happened here, Ord?" Big Al asked.

"Mescalero Apaches. It don't pay to build nothin' out here this far from town. Them darned redskins don't take much to havin' neighbors."

The rider hurriedly rode up in a wake of dust. He pulled to a halt in front of the Bishop brothers, took off his hat and slapped the dust from his shirtsleeves. He was a dark-skinned man of Mexican descent, with a drooping mustache, and two guns strapped to his hips. His raven hair was matted from the sweat of the hatband.

"Right on time, Ortez. Did you have any trouble?"

"No, Mr. Ord, no trouble at all."

"You were able to get the information we need, then?"

"Not exactly, Mr. Ord. There has been a change in plans."

"What change?" Ord growled, his deep-set, snarling eyes flashed at the prospect of something going wrong to spoil his plans for quick, easy riches. "What do you mean, Ortez? Out with it!"

Ortez squirmed in his saddle. A look of fear overtook his face. His discomfort caused an impatient Hale Bishop to place his hand on his gun butt. Ord straightened in his saddle.

"My brother is waiting!" yelled Hale.

"They w-were planning to send the bullion to Ft. Huachuca by stagecoach day after tomorrow. B-but, now they s-say it may be delayed."

"Delayed? Delayed by what?" Ord said.

"Don't know, exactly. Things have been happening."

"What things?"

"Well, for one, a U.S. Marshal was bushwhacked out near the mine. Near killed. He would have died if it hadn't been for that muleskinner Molly McQueen finding him along the trail." Ortez pulled a handkerchief from his pants pocket and began mopping his brow. His hand shook.

"What marshal got himself shot?"

"The one that brought you in, Marshal Kelly."

"What the hell brought him back to town? We figured that phony explosion would keep him away." Ord doubled his fist and smacked the pommel of his saddle.

"Things! You said *things*. What else?" Ord's temper was rising as he had to pry each bit of information from Ortez.

"Well, your man in town thinks it may be getting a little hot for you to attempt taking the gold right now. He hired Jake Strong to gun the marshal, but Strong wasn't good enough. Got himself plugged. Your man says the marshal is asking an awful lot of questions."

"So, who shot the marshal?"

"No one knows. Your man sent me out to scare him away, but not to kill him. I did as I was told. I took a couple of shots at him, then got the hell out of there. But, later, someone shot him for real in the back. But he's still alive, and he's bound to ask even more questions, Mr. Ord."

"What made him come back to Desert Belle?"

"Ben Satterfield's been pokin' his nose into the explosion. Tellin' folks he didn't like the smell of things. The marshal rode into town because of a telegram he got from the deputy."

"Damn the luck! After all our plannin', I don't aim to let no law-dog shut us out of that gold."

"What'll we do, Ord?" Hale asked.

"We'll hold up here until you can get a time for that shipment, Ortez. Come here the minute you find out anything."

"Yes, Mr. Ord. Do you want I should get a message to your man in town?"

"No, I'll go into town after dark and see him myself. Now, get goin'."

Ortez pulled the reins, brought his horse about abruptly, and dug his spurs into the animal's ribs, creating a cloud of dust as he hurriedly began backtrailing to the Gilded Lily mine. As Ortez disappeared, Big Al Barton spoke up.

"How long are we gonna wait here, Ord?"

"However long it takes. I'm not leavin' without that gold."

"What about them murderin' kids?" Hale broke in.

"Let Big Al try cuttin' their trail. Hale, you stay here and make camp. Bill, first thing come mornin', I want you out scoutin' for a good site to ambush them wagons. I'm goin' into town for a visit." Ord Bishop yanked harshly on the reins. His horse came to life with a start as the bit tore into his mouth. With a lunge, horse and rider pounded off across country toward Desert Belle.

The three watched for several minutes as Ord disappeared into the mesquite-covered landscape, then Hale spoke up, "You heard what he said, let's get to makin' camp."

Blackwater Bill was the first to dismount, tugging loose the leather strings that secured his bedroll. Hale followed suit.

"I also heard Ord say I was to track them kids. It won't be dark for a spell. I'm goin' to take a look," Big Al said, remaining in the saddle.

"Okay. But if you ain't back here by the time Ord returns,

you better find another country to live in. This one don't have enough places to hide. He won't take kindly to you screwin' up grabbin' that gold over a couple of snot-nosed kids," Hale warned.

"I'll be back. Don't worry. And maybe I won't be alone, neither," Big Al said. His confident grin showed several gaps where teeth had once been. He pushed his hat back and started back down the trail to where they'd seen the boy's tracks turn off.

Big Al Barton was anxious for revenge.

Chapter Thirteen

"**W**hat do you make of that, Pooder? They're splittin' up, and one of them is headin' our way."

Without further conversation, Blue and Pooder scampered down the hill to where their mounts were tied. They remained just below the crest of the ridge, out of sight of the rider coming from the valley to the east. No trail existed, and they ducked and dodged the boulders, thorny honey mesquite and blue paloverde, trying to miss prairie dog holes and the eroded banks along dry washes.

Pooder found the going difficult as he pressed the old, gray horse to pick his way through the thick and prickly foliage. He swatted at a mesquite branch that nearly hit him in the face, and was rewarded by thorns that dug into his flesh, drawing blood. "Ow!"

"Pooder, you damned fool, you'll get us caught for sure if you don't be quiet!" Blue snapped in a loud whisper.

"It hurts. I'm bleedin'," Pooder whined.

"It'll hurt a lot more if that fella shoots you."

While the plan to stay below the crest of the ridge kept them out of sight of their pursuer, it also meant not knowing where he was.

"Hold up, Pooder, we got to see where that varmint is," Blue called to his companion. "Let's take a look."

Reluctantly, Pooder reined in. He stood up in his saddle and turned around to see if there was any sign of the man closing in from behind. He tugged the straw hat down to shield his eyes from the glaring sun. He saw nothing.

"I don't know, Blue, takin' a chance like that ain't smart. I figure we best just keep on pushin'. He could spot us easy if we stick our heads up over that ridge. Right now, he don't no more know where we are than we know where he is. I say we keep on goin'."

"A half hour ago, you was takin' a nap. Now, you're in an all-fired hurry to git. You just keep going. I'll stay behind to get a fix on that rider. Take my mule with you. I'll catch up," Blue said.

Pooder liked the idea of putting some distance between himself and a killer.

"Okay, Blue, go ahead. Stay low, and get out of there as fast as you can. I'll meet you by that rise."

Blue nodded, handing the white-faced mule's reins to Pooder, who wasted no time in moving on. The ground was rocky and rough, covered with fish-hook and cholla cactus that could dig into a leg or arm and never let go. Blue bent low as he ran, zigzagging, up the crest of the hill between boulders as big as a house, trying to find a way to get to the top unseen.

As he struggled to pull himself up, he was shocked by what he saw directly below his position. The other side was less densely covered with scrub brush and mesquite to slow a rider, and the outlaw was coming on strong. Blue was close enough to make out that the rider was Big Al Barton. A chill went up his back as he realized he was in a tough spot. Barton was headed for the same rise as Pooder. Blue had no way to warn his friend, or catch up to him in time.

As he half-slid, half-jumped from atop the boulder, his hand brushed the gun that hung by his side, the gun he'd taken from Abel Short. He'd almost forgotten about it. He was getting used to the rhythmic slapping of the holster against his leg.

The soles of his badly worn brogans gave little protection from sharp rocks and trail cactus as he ran. Gasping for enough air to keep his lungs from bursting, he reached the rise in time to see Pooder sitting atop the old gray, bent forward with hands crossed on the pommel. Several yards away, Big Al Barton had dismounted, and was stealthily closing in on the unsuspecting boy, gun drawn.

Blue's heart was about to explode as he ducked behind some scrub brush. If either one caught sight of him, he'd be dead. Barton would shoot him on sight, or Pooder would blurt out some careless remark, giving away his position. His hand shook with fear as he tried to gather the nerve he'd need if he was to have the slightest chance at saving his friend.

Although fear ran through his body like a fever, Blue LeBeau knew what he must do, and at whatever cost.

Just as Big Al stepped from behind some rocky cover, Pooder was shaken from his daydream, aroused by some sudden premonition of danger. As his eyes met Barton's, he sat frozen with fear of the bullet that was certain to be coming.

With sweat pouring down his panicked face, he watched Big Al Barton raise his gun and take aim. Pooder fumbled for the gun in the pocket of his coat, only to realize he wasn't wearing it. The coat was neatly rolled and securely tied behind the cantle of his saddle. His eyes grew wide as he realized his time on earth was about to end. All he could do was close his eyes tightly so as not to see it coming.

The smoky blast broke the desert quiet with an echoing suddenness.

Suddenly wide-eyed, Pooder couldn't believe what had occurred as Big Al Barton lurched forward, sent sprawling into the spines of a giant barrel cactus by a bullet from the smoking six-shooter in the hands of Blue LeBeau. Barton hung over the great cactus, his crimson life's blood draining down the deadly barbs. Blue had killed him with one well-aimed shot from Abel Short's .36 caliber Remington Rider. Its new owner had chosen his target well for the first time he'd ever shot a pistol.

"My God! You've killed him! Blue, you just saved my skin." Pooder yelled with wide-eyed glee, shaking with the shock of what had just happened. His fifteen-year-old friend had blown a whole clear through one of the meanest outlaws in the territory. Excitedly, he fairly leapt off the old gray, nearly losing his balance and falling into the needles of a lethal cholla.

Blue stood still, the Remington Rider still pointing in the direction he'd just fired, stunned by his own actions. When Abel Short was accidentally killed with Blue's knife, he had experienced no remorse, nothing. But, this time, the feel of the gun as it bucked in his hand, the smell of the smoke and the flash from the muzzle brought confusion as he remembered the sight of that bullet slamming into Big Al Barton.

Finally, words came, almost tearfully.

"I-I didn't mean t-to kill him, just wound him or something, scare him into . . . leaving us go . . ." he trailed off as if in a daze.

"What's the matter with you? You just saved my life. Probably your own, too. You can't be havin' no second thoughts about a thing like that, can you?" Pooder grabbed Blue by the shoulders and gave him a shake.

"I s'pose not. Damned strange, though, how you actually feel when it's your hand that's killed someone." Blue swung his arm up and wiped dusty sweat from his forehead onto his shirtsleeve. The pistol dangled in front of his face. His nostrils recoiled from the acrid smell of burned gunpowder.

"You didn't go actin' strange on me when your knife killed Abel Short, did you?"

"That was different, somehow. I-I knew he was goin' to kill me."

"It was the same thing here. He was about to blow me to hell, and then you'd have been next. You don't think he'd have just let you sashay on outta here, do you?" Pooder frowned at Blue's remorse. "Weren't never a man needed killin' bad as this one."

"I suppose it *was* the only way."

"Damned right. Now, you're talkin' straight." Pooder hiked up his britches, and reached out for the reins of his horse. "C'mon, we gotta make tracks for that canyon yonder. The others'll be comin' for us when this one don't return."

"Wh-what'll we do with him? We can't just leave him here, can we?" Blue said. "We got no way to bury him."

Pooder shook his head as he started to mount the gray, then, he stopped. He wrinkled his brow in thought. A grin curled his lip as an idea struck him.

"Blue, it's no wonder you ain't rich. You just don't think like a man lookin' out for opportunities. But you just gave me an idea that'll put money in our pockets."

"An idea? What idea?"

"There's a reward for this one, ain't there? I seen a poster on him when we was in Charleston. There was one on that Abel Short fella, too. I'd probably have thought of this earlier, had it not been for the fact we had to get out of Charleston lickety-split."

"What idea, Pooder? You usually get us into trouble with your ideas."

"Not this time, ol' friend. This time'll be different. Help me get this varmint over his saddle. We'll tie him on with his own rope," Pooder said.

Blue slipped the Remington Rider back in its holster, and stood watching Pooder as he approached Barton's body.

"What are you doin'? Are you crazy? What's the idea of haulin' him with us?"

"The reward, my friend, the reward. That dodger said five-hundred dollars, dead or alive. He's dead, and that money is due us. We earned it, didn't we?" Pooder said. "Now, help me get his sorry carcass on this horse."

Reluctantly, Blue moved to the body, but hesitated. Pooder had already grabbed the dead man's legs and was tugging hard to get the cactus to let go of its captive. Blue took a step forward and leaned over to give a cautious hand. Struggling to lift the body up high enough to slip it over the saddle, the two boys were finally able to secure Barton to his own horse.

"We'll take him to Desert Belle and turn him over to the sheriff and collect our reward. Half to you, half to me. Agreed?" Pooder asked.

"Yeah, I reckon . . ." Blue stood thoughtfully for a moment. He surveyed the limp body of the outlaw Barton, draped over his own horse. Then, as if uncertain of the outcome of his statement, he muttered, "I, uh, think I ought to get more'n half since it was me that done the shootin'." He grinned sheepishly.

"But it was *me* that was the target, and that makes us even partners." Pooder nodded to seal the deal with the last word on the subject. Blue, unable to find sufficient argument to counter Pooder's skewed logic, shrugged his grudging approval. They mounted up, and prodded their animals toward the canyon and Desert Belle beyond.

"We sure been lucky, you know?" Pooder said.

"That's the gospel truth." Blue answered.

"It's a wonder Barton didn't turn on you when he heard you cock the hammer on that pistol," Pooder said.

"I-I didn't cock any hammer. Was I supposed to?"

"Of course you did. You have to pull the hammer back or it won't fire, dummy. You just don't remember."

"I didn't, I swear."

"Show me what you done, then," Pooder said smugly.

Blue pulled the Remington Rider from its holster, pointed it at a cactus and pulled the trigger. The blast splattered a hole through the plump, spiny plant, splitting it down the middle.

"Damn!" Pooder groaned. "That's one of them new double-action shooters I heard about. We was both lucky that outlaw Short carried such a piece, that's for damned sure."

Blue echoed Pooder's words. "For damned sure!" He stared at the gun in his hand for a moment, marveling at his good fortune, and shaking his head. The first time he'd even held a gun, he had to go and shoot someone. He said a silent prayer before replacing it in the holster with a faint grin.

Chapter Fourteen

Weak from loss of blood, Kelly had reluctantly taken the doctor's advice and remained at the mining camp two days to regain his strength. It had been suggested he stay a full week. But, he was restless to get back to Desert Belle and learn more about the man who'd tried to shoot him at the boarding house, and why the sheriff seemed so nervous about it. There also was the question of who'd bushwhacked him in the desert. He was up, nearly dressed, and intent on leaving the stifling heat of the dusty canvas building. He was certain if he stayed any longer, he'd be cooked like a rare steak. He noticed his shirt had been carefully mended almost good as new, and he fingered the hole in his black, leather vest where the bullet had entered.

"Well, young man, I see your restlessness has caused you to take leave of your senses. You need to stay down at least a week to let that wound heal sufficiently. If it opens up, you could bleed to death. You darned near did lyin' out there all night," the doctor admonished as he entered.

He knew his words were falling on deaf ears, unheard by a determined marshal who, if he were any other man, would probably still be laying flat, groaning and bellyaching about his wound, not tugging at the bit to get back on the trail of the guilty party.

"I know, Doc, but the longer I lay here, the colder the trail

gets. I've got to corral this fella, and find out why I've suddenly become such a popular target." He struggled with his
boots, but found pulling them on was going to require more
strength in that left arm than he could muster at that moment.

The doctor bent down to help.

"You know that bullet could have been the last thing you
ever felt if it had been two inches to the right," he said, slipping his fingers through the mule ears of Kelly's high-topped
boots, and tugging.

Kelly stood and stomped his feet completely into the black
cavalry boots. He liked the low heels and squared toe. He
never could get used to the high-heeled boots worn by the
cowboys.

"Tell me about that bullet, Doc. What caliber was it?"

"Since you ask, I'll let you see for yourself." The doctor
reached into his shirt pocket and pulled out a smashed piece
of lead. He handed it to Kelly. "I saved it. Thought you might
like a souvenir, assuming you survived," he grinned.

"Pistol, .38 caliber. Pretty beat up, too," Kelly said in studied concentration. He rolled the flattened missile between his
fingers, glaring at it as if it were the unknown assassin himself.
The marshal was beginning to put pieces together as he stared
at the chunk of lead in his hand. First, there was the smell of
cigar smoke; now, this bullet. Sheriff Potter carried a converted Colt Navy revolver, .38 caliber. His eyes narrowed in
thought.

"It hit your shoulder blade at an angle, then nicked a rib
before deciding to retire. You were lucky." The doctor pointed
to his own shoulder blade to give the marshal an idea of the
bullet's trajectory.

"I was lucky that Molly came along when she did. Lucky
this camp had a doctor, too."

"I've patched you up the best I can. You'll be sore for a
week or so, but you'll be all right if you take things easy."

"I thank you for all you've done for me, Doc. I'll try to
take your advice."

"I doubt that, but do the best you can," the doctor said,
gathering scissors, gauze, and several probes and other small

articles he'd left on the bedside table from when he'd dressed the wound originally. He replaced them in his black bag, then turned and walked from the tent with an over-the-shoulder wave.

Kelly strapped on his gunbelt, gingerly tugging at it with his sore left arm. He took up his hat and carbine, and walked outside the musty tent for the first time in two days. The air was hot, but smelled sweet from the wildflowers that dotted the hills where the mining hadn't destroyed all forms of life. A hawk circled lazily above, waiting for the slightest movement on the ground which would set into motion a deadly dive, netting a meal of rabbit or snake.

The marshal noticed his black gelding tied to a nearby hitching rail, saddled and ready.

As he was about to leave, a husky man, clean-shaven and well-dressed, strode toward him as he prepared to mount his horse.

"You probably look a heap sight better than when Molly dragged you in here," the man said with a gravely voice, striding quickly across the open area that ran in front of the row of wood-frame tents.

"I do for damn sure. You Mr. Slaughter?"

"King Slaughter. I'm sorry I wasn't here when you were brought in. I was in Tombstone," Slaughter said. He thrust out a friendly hand. "Terrible thing. They tell me you were shot on my land. That right?"

"Right after I saw your posting."

"As soon as I got back last night, I called all the perimeter riders together. They swear it was none of them that shot you. I believe them. They got standing orders to shoot only if shot at." Slaughter wore no hat, and his thinning hair blew about in the light breeze. Deep lines etched a leathery, wind-burned face. Intense, black eyes stared out from beneath a furrowed brow. He slid his hands into the pockets of his gray, stripped vest. A gold chain arched between the pockets, dangling a fob with a two eagles mounted in the center. The sun glinted off it as it swung back and forth.

It was easy to see why King Slaughter was such a power

in the territory. He stood straight, talked with authority, and came right to the point.

"Exactly why were you headed for the Lily, Marshal?"

"I was told the sheriff was on his way out here. I was stopped by a bullet before I caught up with him, though."

"Wonder why Potter was comin' here," Slaughter mused. He rubbed his chin; his eyes wandered while his mind searched the sky for an answer.

"He may have been looking to meet Ben Satterfield on his way back," Kelly offered as an explanation.

"Back? Back from where?" Slaughter asked.

"From the Lily." Kelly watched Slaughter's face grow intractably dour.

"What the hell was that murderin' Satterfield comin' here for? He knows he ain't welcome."

"The sheriff sent him four, five days ago to deliver a bill for the damage a couple of your boys did to the saloon during a little fracas. You sayin' he never showed?"

"I never laid eyes on him. If I had, I'd have likely chased his stinkin' ass off my land! Potter knows how I feel. He's a fool if he sent that gunslinger out here. Don't know about no hell-raisin' miners, neither."

"You mind if I ask what's got you so riled at Satterfield?"

"He killed my son! Just shot him down in the street. Awww, the boy got a little drunk now and again, sure, maybe shot up some property. Just a kid lettin' off a little steam. They said a stray bullet killed a young woman. If that's true, I'm mighty sorry about it; but it didn't give Satterfield the right to just gun the kid down like a rabid dog," Slaughter's voice grew more and more bitter as he remembered that tragic night. It would never play out as anything other than wanton murder in Slaughter's eyes.

"The doc said you'd be leavin'. I hope you don't mind we got your horse saddled and ready," Slaughter said; the conversation, to his mind at least, was over.

"I'm much obliged. It would have been a real task with this shoulder," Kelly said. Slaughter nodded, then quickly headed off toward a two-story wooden building halfway up the side of a barren, slag-strewn hill. Painted in large circus letters across the false front was: Gilded Lily Mine Office.

Kelly watched the man disappear into the building, then heard a voice from behind call his name. He looked around to see Molly perched comfortably atop the Studebaker's high seat.

"Hey, Marshal," she hollered with a gloved hand cupped to her mouth, "You weren't goin' away without sayin' goodbye, were you?"

"Not on your life, Molly. I couldn't leave without sayin' thanks." He untied the reins from the rail and walked the gelding across to where the wagon was backed up to the open door of a small, tin out-building. Two men were struggling to load four wooden boxes into the back of the wagon.

Where you headed?" she asked.

"Back to Desert Belle. That's likely where I'll start gettin' answers to this," he said, gingerly patting his slowly healing shoulder.

"Then why don't you just climb up here? I'm goin' to Desert Belle myself. You can tie your horse to the back. It'll be an easy ride; give us both some company. What'ya say?"

"Molly, you got yourself a passenger."

Molly slapped the seat, sending a layer of desert dust flying. She laughed when she said, "Then get aboard. It's been a long time since a handsome man sat beside the likes of me."

Kelly walked the gelding to the rear of the wagon, slipped the reins through one of the steel rings on the tailgate, then retrieved his rifle. He glanced at the four small boxes, wondering what could be inside them that seemed to weigh so much. The only thing that came to mind didn't make sense. Gold. Surely, Slaughter wasn't fool enough to send gold bullion to the bank in an open wagon with only a woman driver, even one as tough as Molly.

He took hold of the seat rail and pulled himself up, wincing with a sudden twinge of pain. He leaned the Winchester against the dashboard between his legs. He settled his Stetson firmly on his head, then said, "Let's get this wagon moving, Lady. We've a ways to go between me and that soft bed I'm payin' rent on back in town." She let out a shrill whistle that startled the mules into immediate obedience.

The wagon had rumbled along the dusty road for over an hour when she firmly planted her feet and pulled back on the heavy reins, calling the team to a halt.

"Right over there, about ten feet the other side of that rock is where I found you," she said. "If you want to get down and look around, I've no objection to takin' a rest."

"Good idea. I'll do just that," he said as he eased gently, but painfully, to the ground.

A large, dark, rusty brown stain was plainly visible where his blood had flowed freely into the desert sand. That was where he likely would have bled to death if it hadn't been for Molly. Lucky for him she had seen the black horse standing guard over his master. Kelly tried to reconstruct the events of the day it happened, where the bullet might have come from, and why he had stopped because of the silence and the smell of smoke. Cigar smoke.

Some twenty yards or so in the direction from which he surmised the bullet had come, Kelly found boot prints, horse droppings, and a cigar butt. Whoever had been there was waiting for someone or something. Slaughter had probably been right about his perimeter riders. If one of them had shot him, there'd have been no reason to lie in wait. And, besides, few cowboys could afford cigars.

Chapter Fifteen

As the Studebaker rattled along, Kelly felt he was personally getting to know every rock and rut in the road. The rough ride brought increasingly sharper pains shooting into his shoulder with each mile they traveled—not an unexpected consequence of ignoring the doctor's advice to consider a longer period of recuperation.

"Mind if we take a short break, Molly?" he said. Perspiration soaked his shirt, and fatigue brought on by the pain began to show in his eyes.

"Whooaa, you old flea bags," she called to the team straining at the heavy reins. She braced her foot against the dashboard and pulled with all her weight to bring them to a lumbering, head-shaking stop. Dust whirled around the wagon as the cloud they'd left behind caught up to them.

"Road's a little rougher than I thought it'd be. Sorry for the hard ride," she coughed, waving away the choking cloud.

"I'll live, Molly," he said, patting her shoulder. "Just need a breather."

A short way up the trail, a rider emerged from the brush. A ruddy-faced cowboy wearing heavy chaps and carrying a rope in his gloved hand waved as he caught sight of them. He sat atop his horse with the look of a man who'd spent most all of his numerous years there. A gray stubble covered his craggy face; a quirly dangled loosely from his wind chapped lips.

"Howdy," he called out as he approached.

"Howdy, yourself," Molly answered. "Ain't seen you in a coon's age, Jim."

The man removed his hat as he stopped alongside the wagon, nodded to them both, then wiped sweat from his forehead onto his shirtsleeve. "Sure enough been awhile, Molly. I don't get up to the mine much anymore, what with all these damned strays wandering all over hell's half acre."

"This here's Jim Bonner, Marshal. He works for Slaughter as a drover. Gotta keep all them miners fed, you know," Molly said.

"I think I might have chewed on a piece of your herd while I was healin' up back at the mine." Kelly held out his hand.

"Heard about you gettin' bushwhacked, Marshal. Glad to see it wasn't fatal," Jim said, taking the marshal's hand with a firm grip. "Me and the one of the boys was up to Smoky Ridge that day. We heard a shot. It apparently wasn't the one that got you, though."

"Smoky Ridge?"

"That's where I found you," Molly jumped in. "Top of that hill above where you was shot is what folks around here call Smoky Ridge. The Apaches camp there when they come to claim their share of the beeves. The smoke from their fires clings to the ridge like molasses. That's how it got its name."

"I don't suppose any of you boys saw the varmint that did the shootin', did you?" Kelly asked.

"Nope. Didn't see no one but the sheriff," Jim answered.

"You saw the sheriff on that ridge the day I was shot?"

"Sure did, right up there," Jim said, pointing back the way they had just come, right where Molly had stopped to let the marshal see where she'd found him.

"Which way was Potter comin' from?"

"Down from the ridge. We didn't know anyone'd been shot, though, till we got back next morning. They said Molly had brung in a marshal who'd been back-shot. We'd have surely come to help, but—"

"Show me where you were when you saw Potter," Kelly interrupted.

"We was down in that draw over yonder." Jim pointed to where the land fell away abruptly, just beyond the point where the road turned to the south toward town. "An' we heard a shot comin' from somewhere up in this area."

"What did you do?"

"Well, the noise spooked the cattle a little, so I sent Devers up the rise to find out what was goin' on. We didn't know if it was Indians, or hunters, or just what."

"What did this Devers say when he returned?"

"He said it was only sheriff Potter. He'd told Devers he'd just shot a sidewinder and there weren't nothin' to worry about. Devers said that was a dangerous thing to do with cattle around and all. Sheriff said he wouldn't be shootin' his gun off no more till we had the herd farther up the draw. Gave his word."

"And Devers didn't see anything else? Did he see the snake?"

"Didn't say so, if he did. He come back smokin' a cigar, though, that Potter give him."

"Did Potter say anything to you?"

"Nope. I just seen him ridin' off, that's all."

"Thanks, Jim. I appreciate your tellin' me this."

With a smile and a nod, Jim rode off, back into the brush where he'd come from. "Now there's a job I couldn't cotton to, Molly," the marshal said.

"Why's that?"

"I'll bet when he climbs out of those britches, they stand up in the corner, still bowed." He laughed. She snorted, then, catching his humor, broke out with a roar as she slapped the reins to the team. They came to life and the wagon once again bumped and rattled along the desert road, weaving in and out of the mesquite, prickly pear cactus, and manzanita chaparral. Another hour and they'd be back in Desert Belle. With what he'd just learned from the cowboy, Kelly had plenty to think about besides the soreness of his wound to while away the time.

* * *

In Desert Belle, just as the lumbering wagon rounded a corner, a man stumbled into the street right in the path of the oncoming team. Molly reacted quickly by jamming her foot on the brake handle and hauling back hard on the reins. Kelly was nearly thrown out of his seat. The mules fairly danced on their hind legs as the wagon strained to a dusty halt.

"Hey, you stupid old woman, watch where you're goin'!" the man yelled. His hand dropped instinctively to an ancient Colt Army hiked up high and to the front. He stopped short of drawing the weapon when he saw the marshal seated beside Molly. Unsteadily, he then reached down to retrieve his hat from the street where it had tumbled during his hasty jump back to avoid being ground under the wheels of the heavy wagon. He slapped it against his pants leg to shake the dust from it.

"Now hold on, Mister," Kelly insisted. His voice was stern, but without anger. He knew the man was speaking from the heat of the moment, out of haste and no small amount of fear—along with a fair amount of whiskey. "You shoulda been watchin' where you were goin', and, besides, that's no way to talk to a lady."

"Lady? Hell, that's no lady! Are you blind? That's ol' Mule Molly, and everyone knows she weren't nothin' but a sleazy camp follower!"

"I figure the Lord's the one to judge folks, Mister. And I say you owe the lady an apology." The marshal eased his Winchester up across his legs, bringing it to lie flat in his lap, his hand resting on the brass frame. The business end just happened to be pointing straight at the angry man's forehead.

The man thought for a minute, then slowly backed his hand off the butt of his Colt, forced a meek, yellow-toothed grin, and stepped back. "Beggin' your pardon, *Ma'am*," he grunted sarcastically, with an exaggerated bow. Then, head down and mumbling to himself, he stumbled back onto the boardwalk and into the saloon from which he'd just come.

"No call to get yourself in no scrape over the likes of me, Marshal, but I offer you my thanks anyway." Molly had felt the sting of contempt from men like this one before, but it never got easy to accept. Her usual control gave way to frustration, and she snapped the reins harder than usual against the rumps of the surprised animals. The team jumped quickly forward in response.

"I have a particular dislike for drunks and loud-mouths," he answered. He sensed a deep hurt the man's ill-spoken remarks had brought to Molly. He saw for the first time a different kind of sensitivity in her, more than merely the concern for others she'd exhibited by bringing his bloody, unconscious body in from the desert. This was like a shame, a guilt, some other face she was trying hard to hide from the world.

Nothing was said for the few minutes it took to reach the general store near the end of the same street on which sat Mrs. Dunham's boarding house. As she maneuvered the team close to the porch, she finally broke the silence. "He was right, you know," she said somberly, staring straight ahead.

"About what?"

"There was a time I resorted to bein' a lady of the evenin'. Only way a woman could get enough money together to start her own team. I wasn't always fat and ugly, you know."

"You needn't be tellin' me this, Molly. It ain't any of my business what you did, ever. Besides, you saved my life, and that makes you beautiful to me."

"Thanks. But, I'd still like you to know the why of it. I ain't proud of my past, but I never hurt no one. I did it to survive." She clucked her tongue at the team to move up closer to the side dock. With the touch of a master, she then coaxed the team to back the wagon until its bed aligned perfectly for unloading.

With the wagon stopped, Molly wrapped the reins twice around the brake handle and jumped down. Kelly climbed down slowly. He wasn't quite ready for such physical feats as vaulting off wagons.

"You always been alone?" he asked, lifting the Winchester from the wagon.

"Nope. Believe it or not, I was actually married for a spell. To another teamster. My husband, Abe, was a good man. He was killed by Mescaleros just after turning off Beales Road with a wagon load of supplies for the army at Ft. Defiance. Happened near twenty years back, in '59. He had ten young, spit-and-polish soldiers ridin' guard. Every one of them wiped out. Some hardly old enough to scrape the fuzz off their faces." She sighed deeply before stomping up the steps to the side door of the store. Her wistful look told Kelly she still deeply missed the man. Twenty years was a long time to grieve.

Molly gave a little wave as she entered the door marked "Stay Out".

"See you later, Marshal," she called back.

"Thanks for the ride, Muleskinner," he laughed, moving to the rear of the wagon to untie the black gelding. As he did so, he noticed one of the small crates in the back had been knocked over by the sudden stop. The crate had hit with such force, it had smashed the handle of a shovel that lay in the wagon bed. It would take considerable force to do that much damage, he thought. But, then, whatever Slaughter chose to haul in his own wagon wasn't the law's business.

Chapter Sixteen

Kelly decided to walk the gelding the half block to the stable. After the ride from the Lily aboard the stiff-springed wagon, climbing back up on anything had lost its appeal. Besides, his desire to catch up to the sheriff as soon as possible was weighing heavily on his mind. He headed straight for the sheriff's office after he dropped his horse off with the stable boy, even though the thought of an hour's sleep in that bed at Mrs. Dunham's tugged hard at him.

From far down the dusty street came the thundering sound of a heavy wagon being driven hard. The driver and a man seated beside him were yelling wildly. The sheriff burst from his office to investigate, agitated by the ruckus. Out of the corner of his eye, he saw Kelly approaching and started back inside, but the considerable commotion being raised by the two teamsters changed his mind and drew him back out into the street. The wagon came to a noisy stop a few feet in front of Potter, who was standing in the middle of the road now with his arms in the air. Several townsfolk ran from stores to gather around. A crowd quickly formed.

"They killed him! That's what they done! They done killed him! We found him just lyin' out there, with the buzzards just fixin' to feed off him! It was awful!" the driver shouted as he leaped to the ground from his perch.

"What in tarnation are you yappin' about, Henderson?" The

95

sheriff grabbed the driver's arm and spun him around. "Who are you talkin' about?"

"Ben! It's Ben Satterfield! He's been shot dead!" Henderson cried. Potter rushed to the rear of the wagon. Kelly was only a step behind.

The other man began shouting from the seat of the wagon, repeating the driver's shocking announcement to the gathering crowd. Several people stared aghast at the sight in the bed of the wagon. Potter pushed his way through them. Women turned away quickly, scooping up children who'd also responded to the excitement by trying with youthful zeal to clamber up the sides of the wagon. The prospect of seeing a dead man was too much for little boys to resist.

"I'll be damned! It *is* Ben!" Potter said, turning away at the grisly sight. "Where'd you find him?"

"Like I was sayin', he was just lyin' there, near the road to the Lily, 'bout a half mile down from Smoky Ridge."

Satterfield's ashen face bore the ravages of exposure to the blazing desert sun—burnt, blistered skin, and parched, cracked lips. But, it certainly wasn't exposure that had ended his days. Only the grisly hole in the center of his chest could be credited with his demise. No obvious clue, however, pointed to the identity of the person who put that bullet in the town's amiable deputy.

"See anyone else around?"

"Uh, no sir. I ain't seen nobody since leavin' the Belle this mornin'."

"An' you found him just like this."

"Jus' like you see 'im, Sheriff."

"Okay. You two fellas take his body to the undertaker," the sheriff said to the two who'd brought the body in. Potter lumbered off back toward his office shaking his head. He never acknowledged Kelly's presence. Though somewhat shaken, there appeared no hint of remorse in his cold eyes for the deputy who had served him faithfully.

The sheriff's curiously casual attitude toward seeing his own deputy lying flat on his back with a bullet in his brain made the marshal even more suspicious. How could the sheriff fail to display at least a modicum of emotion at a time like this? To Kelly, evidence seemed to mount indicating Potter knew a lot more than he was letting on about Satterfield, the Bishops, and his own shooting. Possibly a lot more.

The marshal decided not to push Potter for answers at this time, choosing, instead, to follow the two teamsters who now struggled to lift Satterfield's lifeless body from the bed of the wagon and carry it across the street to a storefront with a prominent sign in the window proclaiming the several services offered within: Tonsorial Parlor, Cabinet Maker, Undertakings. A man, peering over the sign at the two making their faltering way, opened the creaking door for them and stepped back, just as they stumbled onto the boardwalk.

Perspiring heavily, the man named Henderson directed the other to move to the center of the dimly lit room, and place the body on a long, bare table situated in the center. Without a word, the two wasted no time in taking their leave.

Kelly had followed them inside, stepping aside as they brushed by in haste to leave the smell of death behind, both muttering something to the effect that they deserved a strong shot of whiskey after all this. He moved to stand over Satterfield, taking mental note of several things about the state of the body that had caught his attention. He heard the floor creak behind him and, as he turned, the man who had opened the door stepped forward from the shadows, his hands folded in front of him.

"I'm Bozell Black. It appears the responsibility to properly dispose of the unfortunate Mr. Satterfield's remains has fallen to me, as it rightly should, considering my credentials. Were you acquainted with the deputy, Marshal?"

"Some. Why?"

"The studied way in which you gaze upon the man suggests you have more than a passing interest; and since he had no kin of whom I am aware, I assume, therefore, that you are here professionally."

"You may presume whatever you wish, Mr. Black," Kelly said as he continued to study the corpse.

The undertaker, clothed in an ill-fitting, wrinkled gray suit,

pulled back the lapels of his coat, tucked his thumbs into the
armholes of his unbuttoned vest, and proceeded to pontificate
with the elegance of an eastern politician, which Kelly felt he
might have been well suited for. "Well, then, I can only surmise
that you are here to determine the cause of his fatality. Though,
certainly without the trained eye of an experienced lawman
such as yourself, I am forced to conclude that the hole in his
chest was contributory. Would you not agree, Marshal?"

"I would, Mr. Black. But that alone doesn't put an end to
my curiosity."

"Curiosity? Curiosity about what? He's dead. What could
there possibly be to arouse one's curiosity? The only ones I've
ever known to be curious about death are small boys and grave
robbers. Nobody else wants anything to do with the dearly
departed. That's why I'm in business, you see."

Bending over the table on which the corpse lay, Kelly said,
"My curiosity has to do with several things, not the least of
which is who would want to see him dead? Also, I can't help
but be interested in these rope burns on his wrists. Looks like
he was tied up for a spell, then probably untied before he was
shot. Rather eliminates the possibility of it being accidental.
And, another thing, take the strange thing that has happened
to his left hand."

"What's that?" Black leaned in to take a closer look.

"His left hand is badly mangled, fingers broken backwards,
like it was clenched into a fist when he died. Someone pried
his fingers open long after he was dead to get at whatever he
was holdin' when he was shot. You can still see the inden-
tation of something round with a distinctive pattern there on
his palm. Deadman's grip."

"Why would a body do a thing like that?" The look on
Black's face had now turned him into one of the curious.

"Let you know when I find out," Kelly said as he turned to
leave the musty room, eager to step out into the clean Arizona
sunshine. "Oh, and I'd like a careful inventory of all you
might find in his pockets. I'll be back, later." The glass in the
door rattled as he left.

*   *   *

Kelly sauntered into the Shot-to-Hell Saloon later that afternoon. The bartender looked up from his half-dozing stance behind the long bar as the marshal came through the tall double doors. The etched glass panels reflected light from the street, suddenly lighting up the inside of the bleak, tin-ceilinged room for a brief, but welcome, second.

"Good to see you back, Marshal," he said, "talk was you was a goner!"

"Near enough."

"You must be livin' a charmed life. First Jake Strong, now this," the bartender shook his head with the words.

"Jake Strong?"

"Yeah. The fella you gunned down over at the boardin' house. That was Jake Strong. Didn't you know?"

"Never heard of him. Who was he?"

"Didn't really know him. I just assumed he was one of those gun-toters that Slaughter hired to ride perimeter guard, or maybe to protect the big gold shipment he's been plannin' to bring in to the bank any time now. But I reckon I never really knew what he did. Kinda drifted in and out of town."

"What about the gold shipment?"

"About all I know is that it'll be the only thing that can save this town from turnin' belly up." He turned to grab a glass from a stack of them behind him, then placed it in front of the marshal. He reached back once more to secure a bottle of whiskey, uncorked the bottle, and poured the glass full. "On the house, Marshal. Figure you need one about now."

"Obliged." Kelly lifted the glass to his lips and swallowed half of the short tumbler.

"You know, we've been waitin' for that gold to arrive here for near two years," the bartender continued, leaning against the back-bar and crossing his arms over his chest. The scowl on his unshaven face spoke for him.

"There hasn't been any gold coming into the bank from the mine, at all?" Kelly found it hard to believe. "So, how does Slaughter make payroll?"

"No idea. But I do know the only thing comin' from the Lily is what the miners arrive with in their pockets."

Kelly stared at the glass in front of him, swirled the brownish liquid around a couple of times, then put it back down in front of him. "Do you hear talk from the miners concerning problems at the mine?"

"No. Mostly all I hear is that gibberish them Mexicans is sayin'. I don't speak Spanish myself, so I don't really get the gist. Fact is, most of the miners out at the Lily is just them poor Mexicans Slaughter gets from across the border."

"He doesn't hire any of the boys from around here?"

"A few. Not many. Not from town, anyway. Say, what was all that commotion on the street just before you come in? Since that wagon come in, ain't no one except them two teamsters has come in here, and they didn't say nothin'. I don't dare to walk out that door when there are drunks sittin' back there. They'd rob me blind the second I turned my back." The bartender shot a glance back at a couple of tables where several empty bottles and numerous glasses covered the tops of tables. Around the tables, men sat, leaned, or laid in various states of consciousness. None looked alive enough to be successful at robbing the till and making anything close to a successful escape.

"They brought in Deputy Satterfield," Kelly said.

"They found him? Is he hurt or something?"

"Dead."

The news brought a look of shock and sadness to the bartender's face. He had obviously found a friend in the deputy. "Damn! How'd it happen?"

"Don't know. He had a bullet in his chest. Been out there awhile." Kelly scooped up the glass in front of him and downed the remaining contents. He dug out two bits and started to toss them on the bar. The bartender held up his hand to remind the marshal that the drink was on the house. Kelly nodded thanks and turned to leave.

The bartender said, "I'll sure miss the old fool," as he watched the marshal step into the street. "Damn sure will," he mumbled to himself as he made a fist and pounded the top of the bar.

Chapter Seventeen

The ride into town had all but turned Kelly into the walking
dead. As he stomped onto the porch of the big house, he was
greeted by Mrs. Dunham's eager face.

"My goodness, Marshal, where on earth have you been? I
declare, you look a sight. Am I going to have to call Mr.
Black, again? He's the one person who I thought would never
set foot in this house before my time. But you saw to that,
didn't you? Gettin' yourself shot at, and pluggin' that poor,
unfortunate Mr. Strong." She talked a blue streak, nervously
tugging at him to come inside.

"One thing at a time, Ma'am," he groaned, as the screen
slapped him on his tender back. "What can you tell me about
this Jake Strong?"

"I can tell you that was some mess you left me to clean up.
Blood, you know, can stain the wood and never come out.
Lye soap and elbow grease! That's what it takes."

"Who was this Strong? What did he do?"

"Now who's asking all the questions?" she shook her head.

"Just curious, I suppose, since I've been shot at three times
in the past four days. Strong?"

"Oh, uh, Strong. Well, all I know is Strong didn't really
hold down no real job. Just worked for whoever would pay
him."

"What kind of work?"

101

"He wasn't known for bein' picky."

"So he was hired to try gunning me down?"

"If I had to guess, I'd say so. Now, let me get you some nice hot coffee. Give me that shirt, too, looks like you been rolling in the dirt," she said, leaving him standing at the bottom of the stairs. She called back, "I'll bring your coffee up. Have that shirt and anything else need's tendin' to." Her words trailed off as she disappeared down the hallway.

He broke into a smile as he entered the small room and eyed the bed with its clean sheets and fluffy, down pillow. A colorful quilt covered the sheets, partially folded down, though he couldn't see the need of it in the sweltering heat.

He sat on the edge of the chair and struggled out of his shirt, trying to suffer as little pain as possible. The bandages cut down his mobility, and kept him stiff. He held the shirt up to the light to assess the neat job of sewing the bullet hole, and was again thankful that Molly McQueen had come by when she did.

Getting out of his boots was presenting another problem. He might just have to sleep in them. He left the wrinkled, sweat-stained, and filthy shirt wadded up on the chair and moved across the room to sit on the edge of the bed. A gentle knock, then Nellie Dunham entered before he had time to respond. She held a steaming cup of the sweetest smelling coffee he could remember. Her eyes grew wide as she saw the bandages wrapping him almost from neck to waist. A slight, dark red stain bloomed on the side.

"Lordy, what has happened to you?" she gasped. Her eyes remained glued to the sight of blood as she laid the cup on the wash stand. Her hand came up to cover her mouth, a tear began to form in the corner of her tired eyes. "I just knew something was wrong."

"Someone dry–gulched me on the way to the Lily. Molly McQueen found me in the desert with a bullet in my back. The doc at the mine sewed me up. I'll live. Although right now, I'd like nothing better than to sample that brew, and get a little sleep." He looked at her with weary eyes. She got the message, picked up the cup, gingerly handed it to him, and eased out of the room. She very gently shut the door behind her.

He didn't show up for dinner that night; instead, he slept straight through until morning. Only with great effort was he able to get down for breakfast. He'd slept nearly fourteen hours, but for the first time since his ordeal, he was beginning to feel half human again.

It was nearing noon as he entered the sheriff's office. Kelly found Potter half-asleep, slumped in his chair behind a table crowded with junk, scattered papers, and an open box of .44 caliber cartridges—probably to accompany the Sharps sporting rifle that leaned against the wall just behind him. The Sharps had a new vernier rear sight, perfect for sighting in on distant targets. But, the caliber was wrong for it to have been the weapon that was used to wound him. In fact, he knew if he'd been struck by a bullet from that weapon, he'd probably be dead, instead of just sore as hell.

Potter stirred as the door closed with a thud. He opened his eyes, one at a time, then gave a knowing nod. "Figured you'd be here before long, Marshal."

"I have a lot of questions that need answers," the marshal said. He dragged a stool over to the desk and sat. "I hope you have some."

"I'll do what I can." Potter moved to pull a dark, tightly wrapped cigar from a box on his desk. He struck a match on the rough edge of a half pulled-out drawer, touched the flame to end of the cigar and inhaled deeply. "Join me in a smoke?"

"No. I just want to know about Strong," the marshal said, taking care to look for any tell-tale changes in the sheriff's expression.

"I don't follow you, Marshal," Potter said, with a long, slow exhale which filled the area around him with a smoky haze. He leaned back in his swivel chair.

"You remember Strong, don't you? He was the fellow that mistook my room for a turkey shoot," Kelly said. His sarcasm didn't seem to ruffle the pompous sheriff, whose attempt at disinterest was all too obvious.

"I told you out at the Lily I knew who he was, and had no idea he was intent on shootin' someone. Certainly not a U.S. Marshal. Why would you think I know different?"

"I saw you jawin' with him not long before he came gunnin' for me. I figure you might have been the one who told him where I could be found, or sent him there yourself."

"Now, just what reason would I have for wantin' you dead?" His brow furrowed in a mock frown.

"That's what I'm here to find out."

"Well, if you're lookin' for me to tell you I done it, you're goin' to be waitin' until hell freezes over. Because I didn't have nothin' to do with causin' that jackal to shoot up your room."

"I suppose your being up on Smoky Ridge right about the time I got bushwhacked was a coincidence as well."

"Now where'd you get such a plumb crazy notion I was anywhere near where you got shot?"

"Met a cowboy in the desert comin' in yesterday. He told me he and his partner heard a shot. It seems the fella with him went to investigate and found you comin' down from the very location I figure the bullet in my back came from. Probably just a *coincidence,* huh?" Kelly leaned forward, eyes fixed icily on the sheriff.

Potter shifted uneasily in his chair. He looked away quickly, took a last drag on the dwindling cigar, then jammed it out in a tin cup that sat on his desk. "You've put your finger on the truth of the matter, Marshal. That's what it was all right: a coincidence, pure coincidence. I *was* in the vicinity of Smoky Ridge that day, but only because I was lookin' for Satterfield. He was long overdue comin' back from a job I had him doin'. I had no knowledge of you even bein' in the vicinity. The only thing I shot was a rattler. And unless you got proof to the contrary, I'd suggest you forget it, Marshal."

The sheriff was sticking to his story. It would take more direct evidence than Kelly had to bring the sheriff out in the open. The best he could hope for was that Potter would say or do something to trip himself up.

"You're right. I can't prove anything. Not yet anyway."

"Now that's the right attitude, Marshal. And to further show I had nothin' to do with shootin' you in the back, there's no hard feelings on my part for the inference," Potter said. He made a motion like he was going to extend a hand in friendship, but pulled back after seeing the cold, steely glint in the marshal's eyes.

"One more thing, what exactly was Satterfield doin' out that direction, anyway?"

"Don't mind tellin' you, Marshal. I sent him out to the Lily to deliver a claim for the damage done to the Shot-to-Hell Saloon by two of Slaughter's miners. That's all. Nothin' mysterious," Potter said with a smug grin.

"Hmm. Reckon you're right. Doesn't seem like much of a reason for murder," Kelly said, pulling his long legs back to stand. "Guess I'll just have to keep looking for the man who slung a .44 my way."

"Now there you see, Marshal, I couldn't be your man. I carry a .38," Potter beamed, pulling his revolver from the holster that dangled at his side, and holding it up. Kelly resisted a strong desire to break out in a grin. Potter may have just made his first mistake, but it wasn't time to let him know that, yet.

"Got any idea why Satterfield was gunned down?"

"Indians, more than likely. That'd be my guess. There's a pretty jumpy bunch of them runnin' around out there. Poor Ben must have just rode up on some renegades at a time he shouldn't have. It's not a good place to be alone."

The obviousness of the fact that the sheriff himself was responsible for putting the deputy in that particular position didn't seem to occur to him. Kelly said, "Did you happen by Black's to get a good look at the body?"

"No need to. Saw the bullet hole in his chest. Didn't leave no doubt there wasn't a thing more could be done for him. I will miss him though, if that's what you were wonderin'."

Just then, a loud, youthful voice called from outside. "Mister Sheriff, could you come outside, sir?"

Potter grunted as he lifted himself from the chair and sauntered to the open window. He pushed the shutters open wider.

Kelly looked past the sheriff, who nearly filled the opening with his bulk. Outside he could make out two young men; one on a gray horse, the other on a white-faced mule. The one on the mule, a black boy, held the reins to a third horse carrying the body of a man slung over its saddle. The sheriff's casual disinterest quickly turned to that of concern when he saw the dark bloodstain covering the back of the dead man's shirt.

"Here we go again," he muttered as he hit the door with all his weight. Emerging from the dusky office, he stumbled into the street.

"Got something here for you, Sheriff," the young man on the gray said.

The sheriff went straight to the horse that had become a pack animal for the deceased, grabbed a handful of hair on the stiff corpse, and lifted the head up for an identification. A stunned realization overcame his face as he leaned sideways for a better look.

"Who'd you say this man is?" Potter said through gritted teeth. His expression was grim, his face flushed. He was clearly not happy to see this particular corpse on the streets of his town.

"I didn't say, but it's Big Al Barton, the outlaw," Pooder said in disbelief of the sheriff's ignorance.

Potter's whole body shook with Pooder's words of confirmation. He was unable to hide whatever it was inside that suddenly gave his face a wadded-up look.

It appeared to Kelly that Potter had not only recognized the bloody victim, but clearly had a fear of this man, alive or dead. And Big Al Barton was quite dead.

Chapter Eighteen

Kelly stepped from the doorway and eased unobtrusively into the sharp shadow of the porch overhang. He leaned back against the gritty wall to watch and listen.

The adobe jail sat alone on the south side of the street. Behind the jail, a steep ravine and dry creek-bed kept the town from expanding further south. A building near the jail had collapsed into the ravine during a monsoon gully-washer that eroded about twenty feet of the cliff. Any thought of further construction was quickly abandoned.

A dust devil swirled around Potter's feet as he stood rigid, fists clenched, eyes narrowed to slits. Big Al Barton's body baked in the sun as it hung across the saddle like a bag of oats. A dozen curious townsfolk gathered across the street, but none ventured nearer.

Potter moved away from the corpse and toward the two boys, who were still mounted. To Pooder he said, "Get down off that plug and come inside. You better have a real good story to tell me." He stomped off toward his office.

Pooder slipped from his saddle and fumbled with the reins as he tried wrapping them around the hitching rail. Realizing he was alone, he turned to Blue, still sitting his mount.

"Well, come on," he snapped. "Sheriff said to get inside, sounds like he meant it."

"Your *friend* can stay here with the unfortunate. You come

107

with me," the sheriff said with a growl, sticking a fat finger in Pooder's face.

"Blue *is* my friend, and he goes where I go."

"Not in here, he don't," Potter shot back. Motioning for Pooder to follow him instantly, he turned abruptly and stormed into his office, paying no further heed to those outside, including the bloody corpse hung stiffly over its saddle.

Blue was reluctant to go into the sheriff's office with Pooder, anyway. He'd never set foot inside any lawman's office and he was pretty sure he didn't want to start now, especially with a sheriff who obviously didn't like the color of his skin. It wasn't the first time he'd been shunned for that reason. You don't grow up in Mississippi, even as a free black, without feeling the lash of folks' tongues who disapprove of your very existence.

Kelly stepped toward the boy.

"I'm Marshal Kelly, what's your name?"

"Uh, Blue, sir. Blue LeBeau. From Mississippi," Blue said with a weak, indefinite voice. Nervously, he reached down to shake the hand of the tall man with a badge and a smile. He'd never had much contact with the law and he wasn't certain how to take one that seemed friendly. The only ones he'd ever known seemed always to be hauling some unfortunate soul off to jail or worse.

"How'd you come on this gent, Blue?" Kelly jerked a thumb in Barton's direction.

"I, uh, well, I come on him from behind and, uh, because he was fixin' to plug Pooder, that's my friend, Zeb Pooder, inside with the sheriff, I was, uh, sorta forced to sh-shoot the fella." Blue's nervousness now broke out on his forehead like dew on early morning grass. His eyes grew wide with the realization of what he'd just admitted.

"You shot this outlaw, Barton?" Kelly asked.

"Yessir. I ain't proud of it, mind you. But since there didn't seem any other choice at the time, I done it."

Kelly just nodded, then removed his hat and wiped his own forehead with a white handkerchief retrieved from his hip pocket. "It *is* a mighty warm day. It looks like you could do with a cooler spot than atop that old mule. What say you climb on down and we'll see what the sheriff and your friend are up to."

"I don't rightly think that'd be such a good idea. That sheriff made it clear he don't want none of my kind in there."

"Well, if you was to go with me, that'd sorta make you my guest, wouldn't it?"

Blue sat the mule while he pondered whether or not to trust a marshal, friendly or not. Kelly said nothing as he patiently awaited the boy's decision. A minute later, Blue spoke up.

"Uh, yessir, I reckon you're surely right about the heat. You suppose there'd be any chance for a cup of water in there?" Blue hit the dusty ground with a thud, wrapped the mule's reins around the rail and, with some trepidation, followed the marshal.

"We'll see if we can't find something to slake a thirst," the marshal said.

As the two entered the office, the sheriff looked at Kelly with a scowl, but said nothing. His relationship with the marshal had thus far been strained, and he wasn't willing to push it further downhill. Blue edged close to the marshal's side.

Pooder cowered on a stool across from the desk as the sheriff stood over him with a menacing scowl. "Now, where'd you boys come across that pitiful corpse out there? And don't try to lie to me, boy. I know a lie when I hear one."

"Didn't exactly come across him, Sheriff; he sorta come across us," Pooder mumbled with a sheepish grin.

"What in tarnation do you mean by that?" Potter's voice crackled with impatience.

"Well, sir, we—that is my friend Blue and me—we had to shoot that hombre before he killed us and left us out there in the desert for buzzard meat. Now, we come to collect the reward. That's Big Al Barton, the notorious outlaw. Rides with the Bishops." After blurting out his story, hinting at some sort of heroic self-defense, his confidence seemed to return.

"Do you really think you can come in here with a cock-and-bull story, and expect me to cough up a fat reward on your say so? Is that what you fools think?" Potter's voice grew louder. His face turned red as he clenched a fist and drove it into the clutter on his desk.

"Folks around here don't take too kindly to someone showin' up with a body what's been plugged in the back. There'll be a thorough investigation before any money changes hands."

"But, sir, ain't it true there's a five–hundred dollar reward on Big Al Barton? Dead *or* alive?" Pooder demanded.

"I may have seen a dodger that comes close to that amount. But that don't mean they're going to just hand over the money to two snot-nosed kids." The sheriff snorted and looked away.

"But the poster just said dead or alive! An he's for sure dead—"

"I think what the sheriff means is that he'll need a couple of days to make out the proper forms before he can get your money, boys. That's right, isn't it, Sheriff?" Kelly spoke calmly, with the tone of a peace maker, since both sides seemed at loggerheads.

"Huh? Why, er, yeah. That's it. It'll take a lot of paper work." He rocked back and forth, frowning, clearly disturbed by the ugly possibilities the body out front brought with it.

Pooder and Blue looked at the marshal for some hint of what to do next.

"Why don't you boys head up the street to Mrs. Dunham's boarding house and take yourself a room for a day or two. Just 'til the sheriff has the paperwork done. Sheriff might even stake you to a meal or two; to be paid back out of your reward, of course."

"Oh, yeah, sure. That'd sure be great with us, sleepin' in a bed and all. Right, Blue?"

Blue nodded quickly.

"That'd be acceptable to you, wouldn't it, Sheriff?" Kelly knew the preoccupied Potter hadn't heard a word he'd said. He counted on it.

"Hmm? Sure, sure," he said, with a wave of the back of his hand, his face twisted into a mixture of fear and confusion as he stared at the wall.

With a jerk of his head, Kelly motioned the boys outside.

He followed them closely, pulling them aside once they'd reached where their mounts were tied. He pointed toward the boarding house as he said, "You tell Mrs. Dunham I sent you to get a room. Tell her the sheriff is payin' for it. And whatever you do, don't set one foot out of that house until I get there, understand? I'll take care of Mr. Barton."

"Y-yessir," Blue blurted out. "We'll be there, sure." He looked over at Pooder for reassurance. "Ain't that right, Pooder?"

"Huh? Oh, yeah." But Pooder wasn't very convincing. Something was going through his mind, and Blue didn't trust that strange look in his friend's eyes. He'd seen it before, and each time he did, somehow, he seemed to end up holding the short end of the stick.

As the boys mounted up, Kelly took the reins of Barton's horse and led it down the street to the same place Ben Satterfield lay—another visit with Bozell Black.

As he opened the door to the undertaking establishment, Bozell Black made his presence known immediately.

"I knew it wouldn't be long before someone came to see me," he said.

"How's that?" the marshal asked.

"Saw them two boys bringin' the departed into town."

"Damned insightful, Black. He's out front, stiffer than a board. When you get him down, see to it his horse gets taken to the livery and fed."

"I'll be happy to oblige. I presume the county will be paying the expenses for this one, too?" A slight nod, then a polite smile came over his otherwise expressionless face.

"Looks like. Unless you can convince the Bishop gang to chip in and give their friend a proper send-off."

"Th-the Bishop gang? He's one of *them*?" Shaken, Bozell Black drew a white handkerchief from his back pocket and patted his moist chin. "You don't suppose they'll be coming here? I mean, with the Bishops themselves dead and all, it doesn't really make any sense for the others to come to Desert Belle, does it?"

"Wouldn't know. Speakin' of the Bishops, were you the one that handled the buryin' and all, Mr. Black?"

"Yes, of course I was. Nothing special, really. They were so badly mutilated by the blast, there was little for me to do except put them in a box and drop it in the ground." He wiped at his forehead before stuffing the handkerchief back into his pocket.

"Was there anything that didn't seem right when you saw the bodies?"

"Can't say there was. Wasn't all that much left to see. About the only things recognizable was their boots." He stroked his chin thoughtfully.

"And what about their boots, anything special?"

"Boots? No, nothing I can recall. Same old scuffed-up, black high-tops like you see on every miner in town. One had the mule ears torn almost off."

Kelly's mind raced back to the day the brothers were captured. He remembered that Ord Bishop was wearing a pair of fancy Mexican boots with silver conchoes. Ord would never have voluntarily exchanged them for a pair of worn-out square-toes.

"Anything in their pockets?" he continued, hoping for some clue that would prove the Bishop's death.

"What pockets? Their pants were in shreds. Sorry I can't be more helpful, Marshal. Now, unless there is something else, I'd better attend to my latest arrival. That midday sun will not be kind to him. I don't suppose you'd know if the sheriff would like anything special? I could make him a real good price."

"I wouldn't know. You'll have to ask him," Kelly said as he quickly turned to leave, wishing that Mr. Bozell Black would not see the cynical smirk on his face.

Kelly headed straight for Mrs. Dunham's. He was anxious to talk to the two boys who'd brought in Big Al Barton. He had many questions to ask, of them and Potter. Along with the mystery of a pair of missing boots—fancy boots with a history.

Chapter Nineteen

While Kelly was tending to Big Al Barton, the boys plodded up the slight incline toward the boarding house. They passed several small, clapboard houses with fences around them made of various lengths of Saguaro cactus skeletons, tied with wire, then whitewashed. Blue thought about how run–down everything appeared, but he was alone in concerning himself with the town's possible successes or failures. Pooder was lost in forehead-wrinkling thought.

"That sheriff is up to something," Pooder muttered as he and Blue approached Nellie Dunham's. "And I aim to find out what. I don't trust him with our money."

"He wasn't up to nothin', Pooder. You're just too damned suspicious of everybody. Now you know what I say is the truth."

"You don't know spit, Blue LeBeau. Besides, how come he never asked about how we come to be hunted by that outlaw. All he was interested in was keepin' us from our rightfully earned money.' "

"The sheriff did seem upset by who the corpse was. One thing for sure, that marshal was set on us stayin' put right here. And he acted like he knowed somethin' we don't," Blue said. "So I say we forget worryin' about the money, and do as he says."

"Hmm," was all Pooder could manage.

Arriving at the boarding house, they tied their animals to one of the few remaining slats in the porch railing. Blue stopped briefly to admire the many wildflowers Mrs. Dunham had lovingly coaxed into survival in the dry, sandy soil alongside the porch.

"I ain't never seen nothin' so pretty," he said, shaking his head.

"Don't they have no flowers back in Mississippi?" Pooder asked with a look of disbelief.

"Sure, but when you been away from beautiful things for a long time, you grow to appreciate them more. Don't you know that?"

Pooder just groaned. It was too much sentimentality for a boy raised with pigs.

Coming around the corner, the two stopped, then gaped open-mouthed at the ponderous porch with its two wicker chairs. The general run-down condition failed to take away from their fascination with actually getting to go inside such a fine house, provided, of course, someone would actually let them in. They marched up the creaky steps like it was their own home. Pooder made a fist and knocked on the screen door. He squinted as he cupped his hands to peer inside. "Hello, anybody here?" he called.

Nellie Dunham came to the door, wiping her hands on her faded and stained apron. She had been in the middle of making dinner and the smells that followed her onto the porch were like heaven to two near-starving boys. "Well, what have we here?" she asked with a broad smile and the always-present Irish twinkle in her eye. "And what might two lads be wantin' with me?"

"We'd like a room, Ma'am," Pooder said, quickly removing his battered hat and trying to sound proper. "The marshal said for us to come here straight-away and tell you the sheriff sent us—"

"And that we was to get something to eat, too," Blue broke in with a weak but pleading smile. The smells of fresh baked bread were causing his stomach to cramp. Pooder quickly nodded his approval.

"Hmmm," she deliberated as she crossed her arms, like a mother about to take charge of her brood. "The marshal, huh? Well, all right, but you shake off some of that dust clingin' to your britches before you come clompin' in here trackin' up my house."

Before entering, both boys obediently slapped wildly at themselves and stomped their boots, creating a small cloud of dust there that slowly drifted from the porch back toward the street.

Pooder pushed ahead as Blue's eyes grew large at the sight of marvels he'd never seen in the poor home in which he'd been raised. Knickknacks sat everywhere; miniature china cups rested on matching saucers with pink and yellow roses painted on them; a small wooden carving of an Indian pony kicking up its heels sat on the mantel over the fireplace; a photograph of a stiff-looking man with slicked-back hair and a celluloid collar hung on the wall in an oval frame; white-fringed doilies clung tightly to the arms of every chair in the parlor. To a poor Mississippi boy, this was a very fine place, indeed.

"C'mon, Blue, get in step, the lady's gonna leave you behind and you'll have to bunk under the porch," Pooder chided as Blue lagged behind, caught up by sights of wondrous things he'd barely known existed.

"No one sleeps under my porch but a man-eating cougar," Mrs. Dunham said with a wry grin.

Blue was so involved with gawking he hadn't heard a thing she'd said. Pooder just rolled his eyes. As they reached the top of the stairway, she led the boys to the room next to Marshal Kelly's.

"This'll be your room. You'll have to share the bed. Now, listen carefully, 'cause there's rules in this household, and you'd best abide by them unless you want to be on speakin' terms with the cougar."

"What cougar?" Blue blurted out, turning abruptly from his sightseeing. He looked quickly to Pooder with a scowl on his face sensing he'd missed something important.

"Shush," Pooder admonished with a whisper, "I'll tell you later."

"Rule one is: No rough housin'," Mrs. Dunham continued, hands on hips, trying to look very stern. "Rule two is: No loud talkin' or laughin' after nine. Rule three: You be sure to wash up good before comin' down to your meals. And you mind your manners, too. There'll be no reachin' across the table— you wait until things are passed properly. Do you understand?"

Both nodded in quick unison.

"Yes, Ma'am, you'll hardly know we're here," Blue shot back. Properly impressed with her authority, and since he was nearly starved, he didn't want anything to discourage the lady from allowing their stay.

"All right, then, we'll be settin' dinner in about an hour," she said as she turned to leave, pulling the door closed behind her.

"Thank you, Ma'am," Pooder called after her through the door.

"What was that about a cougar?" Blue asked, his face twisted in puzzlement.

"The old lady's idea of a joke. Think nothin' if it," Pooder answered with a wave of his hand. He then fell backwards across the bed, arms spread widely. "A bed! A real bed! Can you believe it, Blue?"

The big grin that spread across Blue's face said it all.

The aroma of fresh baked bread, intermingled with the smell of steaming Arbuckle's coffee and the distinctive sizzle of steaks being pan-fried, drifted into the boy's room. It was proving more of an enticement than Blue could withstand any longer. "Do you reckon it's been an hour yet, Pooder?" he asked, roughly shaking the other by the shoulder. Pooder had quickly dozed off in the soft folds of the bedspread. He awoke with a start.

"Huh? Wha—"

"An hour? The lady said an hour," Blue insisted with a nudge.

"An hour what?" Pooder asked sleepily, blinking to regain his wits.

"When we're to go down to eat," Blue urged.

"Oh, yeah, eat. That does sound good, don't it?" Pooder yawned and stretched his arms.

"Well, I'm goin' downstairs whether it's time or not. I can't go another minute without something in my belly."

"Okay, but wait for me." Pooder pushed himself up from the bed, shoved his feet into his boots and started after Blue.

Blue stopped him in the doorway. "You didn't remember the lady said not to come down without washin' up."

"Awww," Pooder protested, "I'm clean enough."

"Not on your life. I'm not gettin' turned away from food just because you don't want to wash them grimy hands," Blue insisted.

With a look of disgust, Pooder turned to the wash stand near the door and hurriedly poured water into the basin from a pitcher that stood nearby. He splashed the cold water onto his face several times, reached for a hunk of well-used, foul smelling soap and gingerly rubbed his hands together, then hurriedly dried off on a towel from a wooden rack above the stand. The towel gave evidence of just how much dirt had collected from a month on the trail.

As they reached the bottom of the stairs, they could hear voices coming from a room down a narrow hallway.

"That must be the dining room, Pooder," Blue said as he pushed past his friend to take the lead, straight for the open door. Stepping into the room, the sight that lay before him was like stumbling onto a goldfield, with acres of nuggets as far as the eye could see. He'd never seen such a long table filled with so much to eat in his entire life. A clean, white tablecloth ran like a narrow trail down the center of the table, and on it sat bowl after bowl filled with potatoes, gravy, beans, and more, steam rising off each like desert brush fires. A fresh baked loaf of thickly sliced bread treated their nostrils to an aroma that gave Blue a sudden rush of melancholy, and a longing to go back to a time when his own mother fairly choked their little house with joyous smells.

Mrs. Dunham entered carrying a platter piled high with meat.

"Did you wash up proper?" she asked, cocking her head slightly and narrowing one eye. The slightest hint of a smile curled her lip.

"Y-yes, Ma'am," Blue stuttered.

"Then you are welcome at my table," she said, a full smile broke on her cheery face. Her graying hair curled atop her head, secured with a wooden comb which threatened to pop out at any moment.

The marshal wandered in and pulled out the chair at the head of the table. He nodded to the boys as he removed his hat and hung it on a peg on the wall. He leaned his ever-present Winchester against the pine china cupboard close by.

The newlywed couple sat across from the boys, holding hands and occasionally exchanging shy, knowing smiles as if they held a closely guarded secret. Next to them, Mr. Cartright sipped coffee as he ignored the others, his nose stuck inside a recent Eastern newspaper.

The boys had little interest in any of others with whom they shared the table. Their minds and stomachs were drawn completely to the banquet that lay before them. "No need to hold back, folks," Mrs. Dunham said. "Everyone's here. Time to eat."

Blue thought those were the nicest words he'd heard for months.

After dessert—a rare apple pie—the boys slumped in their chairs, completely satiated from their overindulgence. As he wiped his mouth with the back of his hand, Pooder looked around the table at the others with whom he'd just shared this grand meal.

"Pssst, Blue," Pooder whispered, bringing his napkin to his mouth for the first time since he sat down. He leaned close to Blue.

"What?" Blue whispered back.

"That man. I've seen him before," Pooder said, staring at Cartright.

"Where?"

"I don't know, but I know I have." Pooder brought his hand to his mouth and pinched his lower lip. His forehead furled as he searched his memory.

"Hey, it's time to get some sleep. C'mon," said Blue.

Pooder got up and followed him out the door, still frowning at his inability to recall where he'd seen Cartright before. He knew it would come to him sooner or later.

Chapter Twenty

As the boys left the dining room, they found the marshal waiting for them at the bottom of the stairs. He motioned them to follow him as he led the way to the front door. Pooder and Blue looked at each other, shrugged, then obediently traipsed after the long-legged man with a badge.

"Don't let that screen slam behind you," Kelly said to Blue, who was the last one out. "Mrs. Dunham is finicky about slamming doors and loud noises." He strolled to the far side of the porch, turned and leaned against the railing. He pointed to the two chairs to let the boys know he meant for them to sit.

"What is it, Marshal?" Blue asked.

"I want to talk to you two about that man you packed in here today. There's questions the sheriff didn't get around to asking that need answering."

"Yeah, that's what I figured," Pooder said, curling his mouth.

"Questions like what?" Blue said with a furrowed brow.

"Well, for one thing, how'd you come to shoot him in the first place?"

"He was after us. Plannin' on gunnin' us down like some coyote or somethin'," Pooder said bitterly. "Guess he felt an obligation to, though, since we killed two of his friends."

"Whoa. Back up, here. Did you say you killed two other outlaws?"

"That's what he said, all right. And it's the truth, too. We was over in Charleston the day it all started," Blue said stiffly.

"Reckon we better start at the beginnin', boys. Who wants to begin?" Kelly crossed his arms and took a deep breath, his expression darkly serious.

Blue looked at Pooder and nodded. Pooder sighed, then began to relate how he'd been braced by Johanson for no reason at all, and then how they'd been tied up to be held for the arrival of the Bishop brothers, and how Abel Short had been told to take them out and kill them, and how he had been killed when Blue fell against him as he held a knife, enabling them to escape. After several minutes of non-stop talk, Pooder finally took a breath. He looked at Blue who was wide-eyed at the re-telling of their exploits of the past few days. He wondered how they were still alive to tell it. He thought someone must be watching over them for sure. His mother had told him about a god who helped the helpless. Maybe that was who it was.

Kelly's face had grown grim. His jaw tightened. "And you say you actually saw the Bishop brothers?"

"In the ugly flesh," blurted Pooder. "They was the ones wanted us killed off."

"How about describing the two men you claim to be Ord and Hale Bishop. Can you do that?"

"Yessir," said Blue. "I'll never forget the way the one they called Ord talked deep like somethin' slimy raised in the bottoms."

"What the hell does that mean? The bottoms?" Pooder screwed up his face. "What're 'bottoms'?"

"Swamps. Bottoms. You know, alligators and snakes. Things that crawl on their bellies," Blue admonished.

"Ain't never seen no alligators. Nor any bottoms for that matter." Pooder shook his head.

"Never mind about that, now," Kelly insisted. "Go ahead, Blue, tell me about Ord."

"Well, one thing for sure, he wasn't never goin' to sneak

up on no one with those boots of his makin' all that racket with every step from them shiny, coin-like things."

"You are saying he was wearing fancy boots with silver conchoes when you saw him just three days ago?" Kelly's eyes narrowed and his expression grew quite somber as he leaned forward and looked Blue straight in the eye. "Are you absolutely positive?"

"Well, yessir, he was. Sure as we're sittin' hear talkin', he had on some kind of showy footwear."

"He did at that, marshal," Pooder jumped in just to make sure there was no doubt about their identification of one of the outlaws.

"If what you say is true, it answers a lot of questions," Kelly said. He turned to look down the street and his eyes fell to the sheriff's office. "It also brings up two more." He stroked his mustache and fell very quiet.

Pooder and Blue felt uncomfortable. The marshal had said nothing more, but they knew something was brewing behind those narrowed eyes, the drawn look on his tanned face. They didn't want to just get up and walk away, not without so much as a by-your-leave. But just sitting on that porch in silence made them both nervous. Pooder decided he'd better get one thing settled before the marshal got any ideas that the boys might actually be guilty of something. He felt the need of assurance that they weren't being considered for some sort of punishment.

"They don't lock folks up for killin' outlaws, do they?" he asked.

"Huh? Uh, why no. I don't think you have anything to worry about from the law," Kelly responded absently.

"Good," Pooder said with a sigh of relief. "I'm feelin' easier."

"Now talk a bit about the Bishop brothers. I want to hear everything you overheard them discussing between themselves," said Kelly.

"You mean stuff besides havin' a deep desire to see us dead for killin' one of their own?" Pooder asked.

"Everything."

Pooder frowned at the idea that anything could be more important than his imminent death. He cleared his throat. "Well, seems they was gettin' the gang together for..uh..what was it, Blue?"

"Robbin' a gold shipment! They was fixin' to hit a gold wagon! How could you not remember?" Pooder winced at Blue's scolding words.

"A gold shipment? Did they say where? When?" Kelly frowned with impatience. "Where were they getting their information?"

"They didn't exactly come right out and say to our faces, us bein' sort of unpopular with that bunch an' all," Pooder said sarcastically. "Of course, maybe they'd be willin' to let us join up now, seein' as how they seem to be gettin' kinda short–handed." He chuckled to himself, looking to Blue for support. He received only a frown for his effort.

Humor wasn't on Kelly's agenda at that moment, either. He let the comment pass, but kept a close eye on the boys' mannerisms. There was a subtle truth hidden beneath Pooder's nervous laugh. Fear. The scraggly kids who sat in front of him knew more than they were even aware of, he realized, and they had every reason to be concerned about their future. As soon as the Bishops found out they were in Desert Belle, and heard of Big Al Barton's demise, these two would likely have no future left to worry about.

If what he'd just heard was true, then Deputy Satterfield had been right. He stroked his chin and nodded. It was a confirmation of what he had begun to suspect. And he now knew the trail to follow. "Where'd you last lay eyes on Ord?"

"It was past them hills to the north, about a day's ride. Near where Barton come gunnin' for Pooder, there," Blue said, pointing in a direction that suggested they may have been no more than ten or fifteen miles from the Gilded Lily mine.

The much promised and long awaited gold shipment from Slaughter's operation to the bank in Desert Belle would come through rugged country, with many places for a well planned ambush to be successful. That had to be the reason the Bishops hadn't hightailed it across the border into Mexico after their escape—an escape that still presented him quite a puzzle.

With long, thin fingers, he began to tug at his mustache—a habit born during times of deep concentration and probably learned from a father with a similar habit of pulling at graying chin whiskers when lost in thought.

"What were they doin' when you last saw them?" Kelly asked, looking first at Blue, then at Pooder for a response.

"Well, it looked to me like they was settin' up camp there in the desert at some sort of an old stage stop to meet some fellow," Pooder said, finally growing more serious about the matter.

"That's right, a rider came from the direction of some mountains that was shaped like a saddle," Blue said. "Over that way."

"That's it!" Pooder shouted. "I remember! That's where I saw him before." He slapped the arm of the chair he was inhabiting, a proud smile across his face. "He was leanin' on a saddle that was slung over a rail while they talked."

Kelly had let the exchange go on without interruption. Now he was lost. "Boys, how about letting me in on whatever it is you're talking about?"

"That fella at the table tonight, the one with his nose buried in that newspaper, he was one of them that met the Bishops back in Charleston when they had us tied to that upright in the stable. Don't you remember him, Blue? Called him J.D.?"

"Are you sure? Absolutely sure?" Kelly leaned forward and looked Pooder square in the eye.

"Positive!" Pooder shot back.

A pensive look came across Blue's face, as he began to nod slowly, trying to put the face with the situation. As he recalled the events of that day, he set his jaw and nodded more positively.

"I agree. Pooder's right. He was one of them," he said, finally.

"This puts a very disturbing light on things, boys. You are in a great deal of danger, so you must listen very carefully to what I tell you to do. Understand?" Kelly brought his fist down hard on the railing to press the point. It was a deadly serious warning. Both boys watched lines tighten around his mouth, his jaw became rigid, and eyes burned with determination. He meant to have things his way.

"What are we supposed to do, Marshal?" Pooder asked. He didn't like the idea of answering to anybody, especially a lawman. He'd never had much respect for them. "All we want to do is collect our money and get out of this town."

"You're probably safer here, where I can keep an eye on you, and on anybody that might be a threat."

"What are you goin' to do about that *hombre* at the dinner table?" Pooder said.

"Did he see you in Charleston?"

"Don't see how he could have missed, us bein' the center of attention at the time," Pooder answered.

"Then more than likely he'll light out of here to get word to the Bishops about you bringin' Barton in dead. I'd better keep an eye on him. He might just lead me to the Bishops. But, in the meantime, for your own safety, you better be sure you do exactly as I say."

"Well, what about our reward?" Pooder pushed. He scooted to the edge of his chair, it rocked up slightly on its front legs.

"My friend Pooder don't think there will be any money, do you?" Blue said weakly, turning to Pooder with questioning eyes.

"Why do you say that, Blue?" the marshal asked.

"Pooder here thinks that sheriff's going to cheat us out of our due."

"I'd say keeping you two alive is more important that any reward. You're going to have to put your trust in me to keep you that way. So, for now, best you turn in for the night. We'll decide what to do in the morning."

The marshal sounded just like his father, Pooder thought. And that was the very thing he'd run away from in the first place.

Chapter Twenty-one

The setting sun cast long shadows that crept across the dusty, rutted street and crawled up the facades of storefronts. Purple shapes silhouetted against the waning red glow was all that was left to illuminate the shabby town.

After seeing to it that Pooder and Blue headed straight for their room, Kelly strolled down the street toward the Shot-to-Hell Saloon. He intended to locate Cartright, and to quench a thirst while he listened for loose talk that might put him on the trail of the Bishops once again. Miners getting liquored up enough to talk about gold, particularly about Gilded Lily gold, might be a good start. For, where the gold goes, he figured to find the Bishops, also. Especially after the boys had told him about seeing members of the gang only a few miles from the Lily. Information on the date of the promised gold shipment would be a good beginning.

With twilight waning, he caught sight of a lone figure walking past the jail. He recognized her even in the disappearing light. Molly McQueen. He crossed the street to say hello.

"Evening, Molly," he said. "Kinda late to find you still in town."

"True enough, Marshal," she nodded. "But the parts I hauled into town today took too long to load and unload. So, I'm stuck here till morning. I'll head back before the sun gets too high."

"Good idea not to try heading into the desert after dark. You might come across a testy Mescalero out for a stroll." He snickered at his own attempt at humor. "Hear they like their scalps curly."

She raised her eyebrows at that.

He glanced over at the pile of reusable adobe bricks that had been separated from the pile of crumbled, useless ones. "Looks like the town council approved the money for a new jail. Seems they've started already."

"Volunteers," she said, her voice almost angry. "Council hasn't the money to approve anything."

"For bein' almost at the center of the biggest gold strike for twenty miles in any direction, Desert Belle sure seems to have hit a snag in its growth." Kelly cradled his Winchester across his chest and started to walk on. "Have a beer with me at the saloon? I'm buyin'."

"That's too good an offer to pass up," she said. She hurried in his direction, trying to keep up with his long stride, her hands thrust deeply into hip pockets. "Reckon it's pretty easy to see, ain't it? Desert Belle's taken on a death rattle. It can't be much longer before she just dries up and blows away."

"Mmmm," he agreed. "Has the town always had to struggle this hard?"

"Naw. Right after the strike, things was lookin' up. The money flowed like water from a spring. Some real nice folks came in the beginning, high on hope and ready to work. Now, most have moved on to Tombstone or Bisbee."

"Why did they leave?"

"The bank, mostly."

"Ahhh. I saw that happen back in Nebraska. Folks gettin' squeezed on loans, lots of foreclosures. One bad growing season and a man suddenly finds he hasn't a cent to his name and the bank owns it all," Kelly said, shaking his head.

"Nothin' like that going on here." She shook her head. "The bank plain hasn't the funds to even make loans. Businesses can't survive without money to buy inventory. And, you got to buy it before you can sell it," she said.

"Doesn't the bank keep all the Lily's money for Slaughter?"

"Supposed to, but Slaughter hasn't deposited anything for many months, now. Keeps promising that big shipment any time. So far, he hasn't kept his word." Molly pulled out a deerskin glove she had tucked into her belt and slapped at her dusty jeans. "I'd quit that bunch if I could get work elsewhere."

"All mines need good drivers. Shouldn't be too hard for someone with your experience to get on with an outfit." Kelly gave her a reassuring wink.

"Men's work," she grumbled. "That's why they all say. Ain't a fittin' occupation for a woman. I was lucky Slaughter didn't care one way or the other who drove his wagons, just as long as they knew which end of a mule to whip."

"You surely do know that. I've seen you work," he said.

"Reckon you have at that," she said with a smile, remembering the day they came to town and nearly ran down one of Desert Belle's notable drunks. Thinking back on how she felt the way Kelly stood up for her made her smile—if only to herself. She picked up the pace and walked confidently alongside the lanky marshal, her head held high.

"Hard to understand why Slaughter would keep the town guessing when he's going to ship that gold. He's surely not worked that mine out, or else why would he keep such a large crew. He's got to be coming up with the cash to make payroll. How's he doin' that?" the marshal frowned as he spoke.

"Oh, he's pullin' gold out, all right, plenty of it, but I can't rightly say how he's . . ." she trailed off as she watched a change come over Kelly's face. A knowing sigh escaped Kelly's lips as if he had suddenly stumbled onto at least one important answer. The change in a man's expression when he goes from speculation to knowledge is hard to disguise.

"He's got a powerful hate on for Desert Belle, doesn't he?" Kelly said.

"Yeah, I guess he does. He can't forgive the town for backin' Satterfield when young Slaughter went on his rampage and paid the price for it," she said.

"Maybe that's why he isn't sending his gold to Desert Belle.

He'd as soon see the town die the same way it watched his son die, then refused to support his callin' it murder."

"But, if he's holdin' on to it, how's he getting the money to pay us?" She twisted her face into a questioning squint.

"Well, I'd have to guess *you* have been hauling it in." He nodded as the idea grew on him. It was beginning to make sense, now. King Slaughter's hatred of Desert Belle might very well manifest itself in the form of retribution by means of economic starvation.

"Me? Hell, all I've ever hauled into the creek was broken parts. You're suggesting he's been sending gold in them heavy crates I've been totin', then it gets put on a stage to Tombstone? And Slaughter has someone in Tombstone put it in the bank? That son of a mongrel is making sure this town dies a slow death. He never intended to help these folks by putting his gold in their bank."

"Makes sense. He figures to let the town suffer as much as he has."

"Trouble is, what he's doin' ain't illegal, is it?" Her pained expression said she already knew the answer.

"No, it isn't illegal. Though I'd say the morality of promising the town fathers a shipment of gold to get them back on their feet, when he knows darn well there isn't going to be one, is on the questionable side," he said, glancing around at the empty storefronts where businesses had already failed from the economic stranglehold gripping the town. "But, legally, he can put his money in an old sock if he's a mind to."

"So, what could we do to teach the lizard a lesson?" She pulled a face as soon as she asked. She was thinking of a little revenge of her own. But that didn't make any sense, and she knew it. Slaughter had given her a job when no one in town would. She didn't owe Desert Belle anything, and she probably did owe the Gilded Lily. Besides, there were a lot of good men at the mine, men who'd treated her decently. Treated her like one of the crew. She didn't want anything bad to come to them. "Uh, I guess I don't really mean that."

"I know." He put his hand on her shoulder.

"We *are* just supposin', ain't we?" she said.

"Just supposin'," he answered.

"It's just that I have a hard time thinkin' even Slaughter would do something so low down." She shoved her hands deeper into her pockets, wrinkling her mouth in thought as she walked.

When they reached the saloon, he stepped aside to let her pass, then followed her in. They took an empty table near the window. The bartender saw them and sauntered over.

"Marshal, Molly, what'll it be?"

"Couple of beers," he said. Then, realizing he'd not given her any choice in the matter, turned to her questioningly. "If that's okay with the lady."

"Yep, fine," she said. "Two beers it is."

The saloon was only moderately busy. Several cowboys from nearby ranches camped noisily at two of the tables as four miners leaned soddenly on the bar. No townspeople were a part of the revelry. Their economic situation had grown too serious to squander money on whiskey or card games.

When the bartender returned with two glasses overflowing with foam, Kelly caught a glimpse of something he hadn't noticed before in the dim light. A gold chain stretched from pocket to pocket across the front of the bartender's vest. In the center, hanging from the chain, was a double-eagle.

"Where'd you come by that interesting fob, Billy? Seems I've laid eyes on one similar before," the marshal said.

"Traded with a couple of miners that came in this afternoon. They offered it to me for a couple of bottles of whiskey. They was pretty parched from bein' out in the sun all day."

"Mind if I take a closer look?"

Billy tugged the fob off the chain and handed it to the marshal.

"Damn!" Kelly growled. "That's one piece to the puzzle I never even considered."

"Huh. Y-you mean you was lookin' for this here fob?" Billy held up both hands like he was about to be robbed. "I-I didn't do nothin' wrong, did I? All I did was to give two bottles for it."

"No, Billy, you didn't do anything wrong. But you could do the law a big favor, if you'd be so inclined."

"Why sure thing, Marshal, what can I do?" Billy looked at the fob with the double-eagle like it was suddenly cursed.

"You can sell me that trinket," Kelly asked.

"Hmm. Well, sounds like you want it more'n me, I reckon I could let it go for the price of two bottles . . . and maybe just a *little* profit thrown in?" With a broad grin, Billy eagerly thrust the object out in front of him.

From his vest pocket, Kelly pulled a small fold of script held with a copper clip. He peeled off several bills until Billy's eyes showed a sufficient amount had been tendered.

"Thank you, Marshal, you're mighty generous," Billy said with a smile of victory, as he turned and walked back to the bar, proud of his deal.

"Molly, I find I've got some unexpected chores to attend to. Come morning, though, I may just ride out to the mine with you," he said. "If you wouldn't mind, of course."

"Wouldn't mind at all," she said.

With that, the marshal tipped his hat and strode quickly form the saloon. Molly stared after him in bewilderment.

"Thanks for the beer," she called after him, raising her beer glass in the air in salute. She quickly downed what was left in the glass, then reached over and slid Kelly's untouched glass in front of her. "Can't let a good beer go to waste," she mumbled.

Chapter Twenty-two

Pooder was lying on his back, hands clasped behind his head, staring at the ceiling, deep in thought. Blue stood at the open window, looking out on the activity taking place in the street by the dim light emanating from the saloon and two or three other businesses that chose to keep hours past sundown.

"You reckon we'll get our hands on any money before the Bishops catch up to us, Blue?"

"I think we should forget about any money and get our tails out of here. I don't feel good about seein' that same man that was in Charleston seated at the very table we were eatin' at," Blue said. "He's in with the Bishops. We know it. Now, the marshal knows it, too. And I'll bet that weasel's here jus' waitin' around for them Bishops to come. Things can only get worse for us if we hang around."

"I'm thinkin' the same thing. Except, I'm not leavin' without our money. We hauled that sorry carcass across miles of stinkin' desert, and we deserve something for it." Pooder lifted himself up on one arm, stuffed the second pillow under his head, then lay back down. "I'll bet that sheriff has our money in his desk, or some place like that."

"It don't do us no good in his desk. We can't do nothin' until he decides to hand it over. That may be never. And we don't have that long to wait. So, I say we saddle up and slip out of here tonight, much as I'd like to sleep in that bed and all." Blue sighed and stuck his hands into the pockets of his well worn jeans.

"You can light out if you want to, not me. No sheriff's goin' to hold out on our money. I'm getting what's due us. And now!" Decision made, Pooder jumped to his feet, tucked his shirt back into his bib overalls, and bent over to locate his boots. Finding one under the bed, he got down on all fours and pulled it from its hiding place. He sat back on the floor with a thud, and began tugging at the mule ears, pulling his worn and cracked boots on over socks so full of holes it seemed foolish to even wear them. "You comin' or hidin'?"

Blue needed time to think this one through. On the surface of it, he saw no way to save his skin but to keep on running. And that was a long shot. He knew that sooner or later the Bishops would catch up to him, and, if they caught him alone, his chances of survival were worse than if he stuck with this reckless, headstrong fool who'd befriended him. On the other hand, if they broke into the sheriff's office and stole money for a getaway—and that's all it would be considered, thievery—then they would have the sheriff *and* the Bishops to contend with. He was in a quandary. A pickle, his ma would have called it. A real pickle!

Pooder wasn't letting any grass grow under his boots as he scurried about, gathering up what meager means he had, in preparation for this chance at his piece of the fortune—or whatever piece he could lay his hands on. And to Zeb Pooder, any part of five-hundred dollars was a fortune for sure.

"I'd like to hear your plan before I decide," Blue said.

"Plan? I don't exactly have a plan, yet, but one'll come to me soon. I'm cogitatin' on it." Pooder continued to gather his belongings as if he were going to leave on the morning stage, and he was late.

"Why don't we just saddle up and saunter out of town. You can be thinkin' as we ride. That way, if you don't get an idea for a day or two, we'll be well clear of here if them Bishops ride in lookin' for us." Blue smiled and nodded, hoping his impromptu idea would meet with Pooder's approval. It was a way of letting Pooder continue to think he was in charge, but would go a long way toward easing Blue's feeling of a noose tightening around their necks—that sense of impending danger he had been unable to shake.

Pooder paid no attention to the ramblings of his friend. He continued on as if Blue had said nothing. "I didn't like that sheriff from the start. I don't think he ever intended to give us our due; fact is, I'm sure of it. I don't think he believed a word we said."

"He didn't look real pleased, I suppose. But that could be because he didn't know us. Don't the law say he has to pay the reward?" Blue said. He started gathering up his few belongings, too, unconsciously caught up in Pooder's activity.

"Law says there's a reward, that's all. Don't say no sheriff Potter got to give it up to the likes of us," Pooder said impatiently. He turned to look out the open window. A slight breeze had begun to stir the night air. It blew the curtain into his face, then, changing direction, sucked it back out the window. Pooder brushed the lacy curtain away on its return trip inside.

"But—"

"But nuthin', Blue! What if the sheriff decides to keep that money for himself? What's to keep him from claimin' he done the shootin'? Now tell me that."

"He's got to know we'd let out a yelp if he done that. Folks saw us ridin' in with that fella draped across his saddle. Besides, the marshal would stick up for us," Blue said.

"I still say he's gonna try to get shut of us . . . somehow. Why I'll just bet he's got that money hid out in his office at this very moment!" Pooder shot to his feet like his britches were on fire, gathered his tattered hat, hung his duster over his arm, and started for the door.

"Now, wait a minute. Where you goin'? The marshal told us to sit tight right here. We ain't supposed to go out there," Blue said with a worried squeak. He grabbed Pooder by the arm. Pooder jerked away.

"Think I'm just goin' to sit here while that sheriff steals what's rightly ours? No sirree! Not on your life." Pooder

cupped his hand around the one candle in the room and blew
the flame out, thrusting them both into sudden darkness.

"How can you be so sure he's got the money? Don't he
have to get it from the bank or somethin'?" Blue fumbled
around trying to find his own hat. He nearly knocked over the
straight-backed chair in the process. His voice strained with
exasperation at Pooder's insistence they leave against the marshal's orders.

"We'll just go on over to his office and take a look, then
we'll know."

"If he does have it, an' I ain't sayin' he does, he's sure to
have it all locked up. He ain't dumb enough to leave it lyin'
around. Don't make no sense, Pooder." Blue pulled once again
at Pooder's sleeve trying to get him to reconsider the rashness
of his actions. "We got to wait for the marshal like he said.
He'll likely even help us get it tomorrow. I trust him!"

"You can trust anyone you like. But he's a lawman, ain't
he? You ever see a lawman you can trust? And I know from
experience that the law sticks together. And so do friends,"
Pooder snapped, again yanking free of Blue's grip.

"I *am* your friend. I don't want nuthin' to happen to you,
that's all!"

"Then help me get our money." Without further discussion,
Pooder slowly turned the knob and eased the door open. He
stuck his head out into the hallway and looked both directions,
then tip-toed out of the room. Blue shook his head, then lifted
the gunbelt holding the Remington Rider from the bedpost,
and reluctantly followed Pooder into the night. A concerned
frown wrinkled his forehead.

They kept close to the buildings, staying in the deep shadows as they followed the hill down to the jail.

"How do you figure on gettin' in there?" Blue asked.

"Shhh," Pooder said, "someone'll hear you."

"Okay, how's this," Blue leaned close and whispered.

"Better."

As they got to the front of the jail building, Pooder crept
up to the only window and tried to see in. The window was

too dirty. He tried rubbing a spot clean, but to no avail. "I can't see nuthin'. Find something to break this window with."

"Nuthin' lyin' around out here. Maybe there's somethin' out back in all that mess," Blue said.

"Okay. You go check. I'll stay here and keep a lookout."

Blue just grimaced with an understanding nod. Looked like as long as they remained friends, he would always be Pooder's fetcher.

He slipped silently around the side of the building, keeping well into the shadows. The first quarter moon, partially hidden by a thin bank of clouds, gave Blue a modicum of confidence he wouldn't be seen as he stumbled along, feeling his way through the dark shadows. Upon reaching the back of the jail, he found himself surrounded by various mounds of splintered wood and crumbled adobe. He squatted over a small pile of junk that turned out to be mostly iron bars from what were once windows. As he reached to secure one of the shorter ones from the debris, he was hit from behind with a splintering blow. He fell face forward into the pile with a groan.

The next thing Blue knew, he was being slapped hard across the face. In the dark he couldn't make out who was hitting him, or, for the moment, exactly where he was. The dark figure spoke with a deep and distinctive tone, one he'd heard before, and it all became clear. A sudden chill of fear and desperation tore through his small body.

"Wake up, you back-shootin' scoundrel," growled the voice from the hulking figure.

Blinking furiously to bring things into focus, Blue could just barely make out another, smaller figure just off to the side wearing what appeared to be a sack suit. Then, he was slapped hard again.

"And if I hear one sound out of you—" the rasping voice continued.

"I-I won't," whined Blue as he held up his hands in defense.

The man reached down, grabbed him by his worn collars and jerked him to his feet. The other man thrust out a scrawny hand and quickly relieved him of the Remington Rider that hung on his hip.

"Now, I want you to get your friend back here. Just call him and tell him you need help. You say one thing more and I'll blow both of you to kingdom come. You understand me, boy?"

"Y-Yessir," Blue said. He could tell by the bitter taste of blood trickling into his mouth that his lip was badly cut. And his cheek was starting to swell from the beating, too. What started out to be a simple search for their just rewards had taken a deadly serious turn. The marshal's warning rang in his brain like a church bell. He was shaking all over as he called out to Pooder.

"P-Pooder. C-come around back. I n-need help," he said. Then without thinking, he tried to warn his friend away with a sudden outcry. "Pooder! Ru—"

A huge hand crashed down hard across his face and, swirling into unconsciousness, he crumpled to the ground.

"Damn, Blue, can't you even do something as simple as—" Pooder was saying with a cry of disgust as he came hurrying around the side of the building. But that was all he was able to spit out before his head exploded in a flash of light due to a hard blow from behind. Both boys lay still in the dirt like pitiful, discarded bags of old clothing.

"Good thing you were keepin' an eye on these troublemakers, J. D."

Chapter Twenty-three

When Kelly went down to breakfast the next morning, the boys weren't there. It didn't seem likely that two starving boys would be late for a home-cooked meal.

"Mrs. Dunham, have you seen the boys?"

"I sure haven't and I've cooked up somethin' special for them, too. Mr. Cartright hasn't come down yet, either," she said, sticking her head into the dining room. "Coffee?"

"Not right now, Ma'am, I've got to find those boys first." Kelly ran up the stairs, knocked once, then shoved open the door to find an empty room.

He headed directly for the jail and a showdown with Potter. He burst through the door with the force of a battering ram.

"Potter! You miserable excuse for a lawman! Where are those two boys?" Kelly went straight for the sheriff's desk where he came face-to-face with the startled, overweight man with a long-unpolished piece of tin hanging from his badly wrinkled shirt.

Potter sat bolt upright from the half-asleep slump he'd assumed before being so brazenly shaken by the angry marshal. In such a situation, most men would have come out of their chair like a catamount to the aid of her cubs. Not Potter. He made no attempt at defense, nor did he make a move to stand. He merely leaned forward on his forearms with folded hands and a look of innocence.

138

"I have no idea what you're talking about, Marshal," he said.

"They're missing and I think you know something about it."

The sheriff's face dropped. "I-I tell you the truth. I don't know a damned thing about them two. I ain't even seen them since they left this very office yesterday afternoon. And that's a fact," he blustered.

Kelly eyed Potter for a moment, realizing he was getting nowhere. Growing impatient for the sound of something truthful, Kelly's frustration suddenly overflowed into action. He moved quickly to Potter's side of the desk, spun the fat man's chair around and glared at him with fire in his eyes.

"Potter, you son of a mule, I want the truth about what happened the night of the explosion. And I want it now!" Kelly said through clenched teeth. Potter shifted uncomfortably, then, with plump hands gripping worn chair arms, he started to stand. Kelly stuck his hand in the middle of Potter's chest and pushed hard, toppling the man off balance and backwards into his chair. He fell with a jolt and a shocked expression. The marshal stepped forward with the authority of righteous anger, the Winchester grasped tightly. The distinctive sound of the hammer being cocked served as a wake-up call to the sheriff. He was quick to realize the time had arrived to come forth with the truth or face the prospect of what was beginning to look like a showdown. Face to face, the possibility of his winning a contest of firearms was out of the question—and he knew it.

"I-I suppose you got yourself worked up so's you just have to know about them Bishops," Potter whined. He gripped the arms of his swivel chair with a near death grip. His knuckles began to turn white when Kelly slowly shifted his stance to bring the muzzle of the Winchester to point directly at the old reprobate's heart. The marshal's determination sent a chill up Potter's spine.

"That's exactly who I want to hear about. And now!"

"Sure, sure. First off, it weren't my fault. None of it. You see, that night I, uh, was asleep in my office when a cowboy come burstin' in the door like his butt was on fire, yelling at the top of his lungs. Said they was tryin' to steal his horse!" Potter's arms flailed the air like a politician fighting for his political life.

"So, you up and followed him out of the jail."

"Of course I did. If there's a horse thief in town, ain't it my sworn duty to stop him?" Potter squirmed nervously in his chair, perspiration erupting on his broad forehead.

"Now, who was here when you left? Satterfield?" Kelly was pretty sure Satterfield was nowhere near the jail the night the Bishops were supposed to have met their maker, but he had to ask, to see if Potter would take any side roads to the whole truth.

"No, the deputy had the night off. Only the Bishops . . ." he paused, then swallowing hard, looked at the floor and continued, ". . . and a couple of drunk miners I drug in for breakin' up the saloon. They wasn't none of them goin' nowhere, so I left with the cowboy."

"What happened when you got to where this supposed horse theft was takin' place?"

"Now, that's the strange part, because he run on ahead of me, and by the time I got to where we was supposed to be goin', he took off into the shadows. Never did see him again. By the time I realized I'd been hoodwinked, I turned and saw the jail go up like the Almighty was bringin' the world to an end. Fire and smoke and splinters flyin' through the air thicker'n fleas on a mongrel. Bright as the damned noonday sun!" Potter's arms flew up as his eyes grew wide. Kelly thought that as soon as the sheriff's lawman days came to an end—which he hoped would be soon—he'd likely have a great future as a storyteller. Though this was undoubtedly the first real emotion he'd seen Potter display since arriving.

"I ran back to the jail . . . and that's when I seen 'em all blowed to pieces . . . it was the grisliest mess I'd ever laid eyes on." Potter buried his head in his hands.

"How many were there in the rubble?"

"Just two of 'em. That's when I knew how bad I'd been suckered. I knew immediately it wasn't them Bishops. The cell they was in was empty. One of their gang musta slipped in, let them out, then planted an explosive right in their empty cell. When I realized they was gone, hell, I was scared near to death."

"So you decided not to tell anyone about the Bishops' escape, figuring to just forget those poor miners and let the town think you'd just let them off with a warning."

"No one even knew I'd put 'em up for the night. Not even Satterfield." Potter's voice was weak as he heard the truth of his crime out loud for the first time.

"So, when Slaughter just assumed they'd drifted off, rather than face a dressing down for getting drunk and tearing the saloon apart, you figured to just let him think it. Never bothered to set him straight. Sent Satterfield out to collect for the damages because you couldn't look Slaughter in the face, figuring he'd know you was lyin'. That about it?"

"About it," Potter mumbled, head hung down, staring at a knothole in the floor. "If the town board found out I'd let the likes of them Bishops get away, I'd been lookin' for a new job."

"You work too hard keepin' the job and not hard enough keepin' the law."

The room fell silent as Kelly watched the torment on the sheriff's face wrinkle and age him as he slumped further in his chair.

"You're the one who bushwhacked me, aren't you?"

"Yeah," Potter said barely above a whisper. "I figured it was only a matter of time before you put it all together. I needed you out of the way for a spell to give me some time to get it all worked out. I never meant to hit you, just scare you off, maybe keep your mind off the Bishops for awhile. My eyesight ain't what it used to be."

"How'd you figure to work it out?"

"I-I'm not sure . . . maybe get lucky, or something."

"You send Jake Strong to gun me?"

"No! I told you, he just said he wanted to talk to you about something. I pointed the way, that's all. I swear."

If Potter didn't point Strong in my direction, then there's

more than one skunk tryin' to bag himself a marshal, Kelly thought. He stroked his chin for a moment, not entirely certain about the veracity of the sheriff's claim of innocence in the matter.

"I don't suppose you'd have any idea who did send him," the marshal said. His voice was full of contempt.

"No idea at all."

"You have anything to do with killing Satterfield?"

"Hell no! He was a good man. Near broke my heart to see him lyin' there with that bullet in his chest."

"You have a strange way of showing sorrow, old man."

Potter sank a little deeper into his chair.

"You're a pitiful excuse for a lawman, Potter. I'd say your days as a sheriff anywhere in Arizona are over. But, you might just escape going to prison for drygulching a U.S. Marshal if you cooperate with me in stopping the Bishops once and for all. Interested?"

Potter's eyes showed a spark of life as they came slowly up from the floor to finally look the marshal in the face. "What's your offer?"

"First off, you're going to help me find those two boys. And I can tell you one thing, they better be in damned good shape or . . ." Kelly released the hammer on the Winchester and slapped the fore stock in his hand. He decided to let Potter chew on what might await him if Pooder and Blue weren't still alive. If Potter had anything to do with their disappearance, he'd probably make a beeline for where they were, alive or not. Kelly wasn't certain he dared to let the sheriff out of his sight. But, since he had no one else to watch his back, having Potter along seemed the only alternative. He'd just have to be very watchful.

Of course there was a possibility that Potter actually didn't know anything about the boys' sudden departure. In which case time was being wasted standing around jawing with the sheriff.

"I'm going to take a chance on you, Potter. Get your horse saddled and ready for a ride. Come armed. We'll leave in fifteen minutes. Oh, one more thing, Sheriff, if you don't show up, you better be dead."

Kelly pondered the whole situation as he saddled the big gelding. On his way to the stable, he ran into Molly. She told him she'd just learned that the gold shipment was supposed to be coming tomorrow. King Slaughter was making sure the whole town knew of his plans. It made sense that the Bishops knew also. They'd probably be planning to hit the wagons somewhere along the most desolate stretch of road between the Lily and Desert Belle, a winding five miles with more natural opportunities for an ambush than a blind canyon.

It was now up to him to stop the Bishops, even though he figured there was no gold being shipped anyway. Kelly saw the whole thing as another ploy by Slaughter to get the town's hopes up, then see their suffering turn to despair when the wagons failed to get through. He'd blame it all on the Bishops, who, by then, would be trying for a clean getaway with several crates of rocks or broken machine parts. Any of the mine's men killed or wounded in the attack would be expendable.

Fifteen minutes later, when Kelly arrived at the jail, Potter was mounted and ready on the back of a gray mare that looked as if she'd expire if they were out more than a couple hours.

"Where are we headed?" Potter asked.

"Out there," Kelly said as he pointed in the general direction of the Lily. "If, as you claim, you had nothing to do with their disappearance, I have an idea where they may be and who they might be keeping unwilling company with."

"Who?" Potter sad.

"Your old friends, the Bishops."

Potter's eyes widened and his face turned pale. He swallowed hard as he removed his drooping, filthy hat and wiped his forehead with his shirt sleeve.

Kelly smiled to himself as he clucked the gelding forward. Potter fell in behind with a look of despair as he slumped in the saddle.

Chapter Twenty-four

"Glad you're back, Ord," Hale said. "I'm getting a mite fidgety."

"Long ride. Near a full day. Worth it, though." Ord Bishop dropped his saddle near the small campfire. He tossed his sweat-stained hat onto the saddle horn and ran his fingers through his thinning hair.

"What happened in Desert Belle? Where's Big Al? How'd you come by them two?" Hale threw a thumb over his shoulder to indicate the two trussed-up and unconscious captives Ord and J.D. had brought with them.

"Just hold your britches, I'll tell you the whole story," Ord said. He stared at his brother for a moment, then his stolid expression changed to one of grief. "You should have seen him. They brung him into town throwed over his own saddle, a hole clean through him. It was a pitiful sight, I tell you! And them's the ones done it!"

"What the hell you talkin' about? Who got shot?" Hale's confusion over his brother's babbling brought an angry scowl to his face.

"Big Al! You damned fool, didn't you wonder where he'd got to?"

Hale shifted his weight from one leg to the other, embarrassed by his condemnation, but anxious to get the whole story. "Now just how'd them two scraggly kids ever get the drop on Big Al, anyway? Answer me that."

"How am I supposed to know? Luck, I reckon, pure dumb luck. But don't you fret, it's our turn, now. Things are about to turn around for the Bishop bunch, damned if they ain't," Ord said with gritted teeth and narrowed eyes.

"Amen to that," Hale said.

Blue couldn't understand why, struggling as hard as he could, he found it impossible to raise either hand to rub his throbbing head. He thrashed about but a rope was wound so tightly around him that freedom was hopeless. His struggles were to no avail and he began to feel panic.

As he slowly drifted back to the surface of consciousness, he felt a wave come over him like he was going to vomit. He ached all over. It even hurt to open his eyes, but he forced himself to. Then, he wished he hadn't.

The light was dim, but he could make out three figures squatted near a campfire several yards away. They seemed to be in heated argument over the fate of "them two bastards over there in the bush." That, he assumed, would be him and Pooder. If his fate was being decided by the same man who knocked him down in back of the jail, he knew what that fate was to be. His goose was cooked. And Pooder, too, was a goner. If he wasn't already.

Blue tried to roll over, but found himself securely bound, hands and feet, hog-tied, and unable to get off his belly. Being unable to move had led to a feeling of panic as he regained consciousness. Then, he heard groaning to his right.

"Pooder, that you?" Blue whispered.

Another groan. Then a muffled grunt like someone trying to talk with a mouthful of mud.

"Pooder!" Blue said again.

"Uh-huh, hmmm," came the incoherent answer.

"Pooder, if you can hear me, we're in a heap of trouble."

No answer.

"Pooder! You've got to wake up! You got us in a real mess this time. The Bishops got us! Can you hear me?"

After more than a minute of spitting and mumbling, Pooder was finally able to mumble a few, almost intelligible words. "I got a mouthful of the godawfulust stuff I ever seen. I got to get me a drink."

More unrecognizable mumbling came from where Blue figured Pooder to be. He assumed his friend must be tied in much the same manner as he was. He must have been whumped over the head the same, too, since he had heard mostly gibberish from the barely visible form off in the brush several feet away. He felt a surge of anger that Pooder kept making such dumb mistakes. If only they'd listened to the marshal, none of this would have happened.

"Pooder!" he tried once more.

"Uh-huh," groaned the wriggling mass from the darkness.

"Can you talk? Are you hurt?"

"Some, I think. Hurt, I mean." Pooder spit out more dirt. "Can't get free enough to tell, but my head feels like it's going to explode."

"Me, too. Listen, keep your voice down, they're right over there a ways. It's them Bishops, and I think they're plannin' how to get shut of us for good. We got to get out of here somehow. I don't suppose you got any great ideas?" Blue said with obvious sarcasm.

"Un-uh," was all that came from Pooder's mouth.

Just then, Blue heard footsteps in the gravel, approaching from the direction of where the outlaws had been huddled. He struggled to turn his head to see what was going on when he saw the leader, Ord Bishop, coming toward him. He froze.

"Well, well, I see you finally woke up, you fool kid. Thought there for a time I mighta hit you too hard with that stump of lumber. Lucky you got a hard head." Ord stood over Blue, glaring at him with fire in his cruel eyes.

"Wh-what you gonna do with us?" Blue said weakly.

"At first, I was going to string you up. Watch you blow in the wind, kickin' and chokin', then drag your bodies through the cactus. But, I come up with a better idea: you two are going to get blown to high heaven while helpin' us rob a gold wagon." Ord laughed even harder. "You know, I think Johanson, Big Al and ol' Abe would like the idea of seein' parts of two scrawny, lily-livered backshooters scattered all over the countryside."

He turned and started to rejoin the others, but stopped a few feet away and turned back. "Hope you ain't hungry nor nuthin', I ain't got none to spare. Water neither. Ha!"

He stomped off whistling.

Blue's heart sank.

"Who was that you was talkin' to?" Pooder said.

"Ord Bishop. Says he's gonna blow us up. Leave our bodies spread all across the county."

"Oh." Pooder sounded as if he wished he hadn't asked. From off in the distance, the roar of something like canon fire filled the night air. "Sounds like they're already practicin'."

"That's just thunder. A storm's comin'."

"Oh, that's all I need, getin' drowned at the same time I'm gettin' blowed up."

Ord re-joined the others at the small campfire. The fire wasn't for keeping warm, the desert sand and gravel held enough heat to keep a man comfortable all night in the summer. This fire was to heat coffee and cook the jackrabbit Hale had shot earlier that afternoon as he waited for Ord to return.

"Heard in town them ore wagons is supposed to roll tomorrow. That goes along with the word you got from Ortez this morning, Hale, so here's the plan." Ord squatted on his haunches, pulled a small mesquite twig from a pile near the fire, and started to draw in the sand. Hale and J.D. Cartright moved closer. Ord made an "X" with the twig. "Blackwater Bill's out scoutin' a site. Now, here's how we'll set the ambush."

"How many wagons you figure there'll be?" Hale asked.

"Two, maybe three. And an armed driver and three guards for each wagon."

"That's eight to twelve men, Ord, how's the four of us goin' to take that many? Especially with *him* bein' no hand with a gun." Hale hooked a thumb towards Cartright, a concerned look on his weather–beaten face.

"Hell, we got them two back there in the brush, they's gonna help," Ord said with a smirk. J.D. Cartright and Hale looked at each other, then broke out in laughter.

"This ain't no time for no jokes, big brother," Hale said. "We're serious." He nodded toward J.D.

"So am I," Ord said. He continued to draw in the sand. "Here's the route we'll take to intercept 'em. Here's where we'll hit 'em. And here's our route of escape."

"How we gonna carry all that gold out of there?"

"The same way it came—on their own wagons."

"I don't get it!" Hale interrupted. "After J.D. gets through with that nitro you told him to bring, there ain't gonna be much left of them wagons but splinters."

"The explosion ain't for the wagons, it's for the men around the wagons. That's the reason we're going to use nitro instead of dynamite—much greater shock. It'll send a man flying right off a horse thirty feet away."

"I still don't understand," Hale said.

"With dynamite, you have to light a fuse, right?"

"Yeah."

"And you can only guess exactly when it's gonna go off."

"Reckon that's true, too."

"With nitro, we get a bigger bang, and it goes off right when we want." Ord smiled with satisfaction at the simplicity of his plan.

"How's it goin' to do that?" Hale said, frowning that he still seemed to be missing something.

"We stick them two back shooters in the middle of the road, tied to each other so they can't move, and gagged so they can't call out no warnin'. We set two bottles of nitro between them, and a couple near the roadside just for good measure. When the wagons approach, they'll slow down so's they don't run over the unfortunate lads. The guards will come up to see what's goin' on, and we fire a shot at the nitro. Whooom! Whoom! One after another. Them bastards back there are scattered over the sand like snow, and the guards are so dazed we pick them off like shooting chickens in a coop, and we're richer by a million dollars worth of gold. You get the idea, baby brother?"

Hale was grinning from ear to ear. J.D. seemed to light up at the explanation, too. Hale lit a quirly from a burning stick he pulled from the fire, them took a long, satisfying drag of smoke.

"Now, it's important we get them wagons rollin' out of there quick. That blast will be heard all the way into Desert Belle and even that stupid sheriff is bound to come lookin' to see what the noise is all about. That damned marshal, too, no doubt. So no time for celebratin' til we get the bounty hidden," Ord said.

"Where we goin' to hide the gold?" J.D. said.

"I got that all figured out. Found a place hid up in them hills to the south. They'll not be followin' us too far into the brush. Mescalero country."

"What makes you think we aren't takin' the same chances?"

"I promised the Apaches some new rifles. They'll want us alive . . . at least until we deliver those carbines."

"When'll that be?" Hale asked.

"Never! Ha ha!"

Hale turned to J.D. with a worried look. J.D. just shrugged, then, picking up a small stone, tossed it into the brush and said, "You know Ord, I ain't never been much with a gun. You *sure* you wouldn't rather find someone to take my place?"

Ord's face twisted into an angry fist. "Hell yes, I'd rather have a real gun out there, but them two bastards we got trusted up back there done killed them all! I got no damned choice!" He jumped to his feet and kicked dirt on the fire, quenching it. He stomped over to where his saddle lay, tore the bedroll from the back of it, and threw it in the dust. "Now, get some sleep! We ride at sunup!"

After the campfire was out, Blue waited until the three outlaws were snoring loudly before trying to talk to Pooder any further. They had to come up with a plan of escape. They always had before. But now, time was very short and they weren't just up against a couple of loud mouths like Johanson or Abel Short; now they would have to match wits with the Bishops themselves. Blue knew they were overmatched. It would take some sort of a miracle to survive this predicament.

"Pooder, you awake?" Blue whispered.

"Yeah." Pooder's tone was forlorn, hollow.

"They took my gun. Did they get yours, too?"

"I reckon. My slicker's gone. Besides, I can't even move my little toe I'm so wound up in rope. Doubt I could pull a trigger if I had my finger on one."

"Then I reckon our time's up," Blue groaned. He thought he heard Pooder swallow hard just then.

Chapter Twenty-five

As Kelly and Potter slowly rode farther into the desert, Kelly's thoughts were a grab bag of questions: How and where will the Bishops strike the wagons from the Lily? How can a man like King Slaughter keep carrying so much hate he'd make a whole town pay for the righteous shooting of his son? And who sent Jake Strong to shoot him at the boarding house?

As much as it irritated him to ask, he knew Potter had answers to some of his questions, probably without even knowing it.

"If you were aimin' to set up an ambush, where would you likely do it?" Kelly said.

"If I had twenty, thirty men with me, I'd probably be waitin' at Dry River Bend. Catch 'em off guard as they come around where the cliffs rise up high. That way there wouldn't be no place to turn around or run for it," Potter answered.

"What if the whole gang were only a handful, say three or four? That make a difference?"

"I doubt them Bishops will hit those wagons with no more guns than that. Hell, the Lily will have ten, maybe twelve men guardin' that shipment." Potter shook his head.

"But what if they had no choice?" Kelly wasn't getting the answers he wanted out of Potter. The stubborn old sheriff just couldn't think like a lawman, even after all his years of experience.

"No choice? Why'd that be?"

"Look, that gang was made up of the same bunch as long as I can recall. Abel Short, Eb Johanson, and Big Al Barton were killed by those boys. I shot K.D. Keyes. That leaves Blackwater Bill DeMotte, and the two Bishops. There may be a fourth one if you count whoever they have in town feeding them information."

"Now who'd that be?" Potter said.

"Pretty sure it's that so-called salesman at the boarding house, J.D. Cartright. Boys said they saw him with the Bishops over in Charleston," Kelly said.

"I sure never knowed about him," Potter said with a frown, shaking his head. "I'm gettin' too old for this."

"For a spell, I thought it might be you."

Potter hung his head. "Reckon I had that coming."

They rode on for another mile or so before Kelly restated his original question. "I still haven't heard your opinion on where they'll likely strike."

"Oh, yeah. Well, if it's as you say, I s'pose I'd hunker down somewhere along the dusty flats, just south of Smoky Ridge." Potter pulled a cigar out of his shirt pocket, bit off the end and spit it out, then sniffed the tobacco before putting it in his mouth.

"Smoky Ridge, huh? Hmmm. Does seem a good place for an ambush, all right," Kelly said with a hard glance at the sheriff.

Potter looked away quickly.

"One more thing, do you know where there's an old abandoned stage stop somewhere south of that ridge of hills yonder?" Kelly asked.

"Sure."

"Lead the way, then, because you're takin' us there."

"Why in tarnation would we be traipsin' off to see a couple of crumbling buildings taken over by cactus and coyotes?" Potter shifted in his saddle, trying to understand what gave the marshal such a fool notion. He was more interested in making camp, getting out of an uncomfortable saddle and into a bedroll. He'd been atop that swayback nag for most of ten hours already. It was getting onto evening, the sun had taken refuge behind several gathering thunderheads building over the mountain range to the west. Sure as sunrise, they were going to get drenched before the night was out. The sheriff was keenly aware that riding blindly around the desert in the pitch black during a thunderstorm was a good way to get swept into the other world in a flash flood or cooked to charcoal in a lightning strike. Concern over the situation turned his thick, dark eyebrows into a pair of brooding vultures perched on a wrinkled ledge above a large, slightly crooked nose. As if that weren't enough, Potter had something new to worry about at Kelly's next words.

"That's where I figure the Bishops are. And, if we aren't already too late, I figure they have two foolish boys with them who wouldn't be there if they'd listened to orders. Nevertheless, I want them back safe, and before the shooting starts."

After hearing that, Potter grew even more restless over the next hour as they rode toward the possible camp of the Bishop gang. Finally, he could remain silent no longer.

"You of all people should know, Marshal, I, uh, ain't much with a gun no more. Maybe you should go in there alone, so I don't become a hindrance and end up shootin' my own foot off, or something."

"You're going where I go. Might as well get used to it."

Just then, Kelly held up his hand and reined in his horse. Potter did the same. Kelly stood up in his stirrups, straining to see something in the distance.

"Over there, Potter, do you see that glow? Looks like a campfire."

Potter stared in the direction the marshal was pointing, but just shook his head. "I don't see nothin'. These old eyes ain't too good at distances. But the old stage depot does lie in that general direction, no more than a mile or so from here."

"Okay, let's keep moving." Kelly clucked his tongue and the gelding responded instantly.

Darkness was overtaking them much faster than they expected because of the approaching thunderstorms. Towering buildups of boiling clouds imitated great dark mountains on the move. Thunder echoed across the desert like giant cannons firing and lightning shot through the gathering blackness, striking the ground in explosive bursts of dazzling light.

Potter's horse was showing signs of increasing nervousness as the storm drew closer. "Maybe we ought to find shelter and wait out the storm," the sheriff said.

"The rain'll give us cover while we get close to their camp. How much farther?"

"Not far. Hundred yards or so," Potter said, catching a glimpse of a landmark by the flash of a lightning bolt.

"Good a time as any to dismount, then, and tie the horses up in that stand of mesquite over there," Kelly said, pointing to a thicket of the spiny trees a few yards behind them. "We'll go the rest of the way on foot."

Potter wanted out of that saddle worse than anything. He voiced no objections to Kelly's order.

The rain had started and the boys were trembling in the sudden coldness of the storm. They were totally unprotected and the water soaked through their clothing quickly. Shivering and scared, Blue called out, for little more reason than to hear another voice.

"Pooder! You still there?"

" 'Course I'm still here, you idjit! Where'd I go trussed up like a hog to market?"

"Just thought you might'a come onto a plan of escape by now. You been quiet an awful long time."

"Well, I ain't come up with nothin'." Pooder again fell silent.

Blue continued to struggle with his ropes. It was no use, the pelting rain was only making them tighter. He thought of Mississippi and how some white boys had tied him to a stump for a joke. He was able to free himself after about an hour by rubbing the ropes up and down against the rough bark. The joke had been on them when he snuck into town and found them gathered behind the stable sneaking a smoke. He tied their horses' reins together in such a knot, they had to cut them apart to get home. Each of them got a licking. After that, they didn't pick on the little black boy from the cotton patch any more.

Straining with all his might, he was unable to even roll over let alone find something to rub his binds against. After many hours, it had become apparent there would be no such escape this time. The rough ground where his face lay was no longer dirt and sand. It was now mud and sand. Tears began to flow, adding to the growing puddle.

The only light Kelly and Potter had to guide them to their destination was the staccato flashes of lightning that gave a sudden, but short-lived, midday brilliance to the cactus-strewn landscape.

"Keep going, Potter, but stay down so they don't spot us before we see them," Kelly whispered as he put a wet hand on the sheriff's shoulder.

"I think the old depot is right over there," Potter said. He wiped the rain out of his eyes and pointed to another small rise in front of them. "What do we do now?"

"First, I want to locate where they've got those boys, assuming they're still alive."

Just then a crash of thunder nearby brought a shout from someone. It sounded as if it came from only a few feet away. Both lawmen hit the ground at the same time to avoid being seen. Just then, two of the gang passed close by.

"Darn it, Bill, make sure the horses are secure. Can't have them gettin' spooked with that nitro in the saddle bags."

"Maybe we ought to unload it and put it in the ruins until the storm's over, Ord."

The exchange between the two continued, but they had lowered their voices enough that Kelly could no longer make out what was being said. He pulled Potter close and whispered, "Guess there's no more doubt about the Bishops being alive."

"Reckon not," came a very humble, hushed reply. "What now?"

"I'm goin' up there to the top of that rise and get a better look at the layout. I want you to stay low, move around the edge of this ravine, see if you can locate the boys. If you can, and you can get to them, try to free them and get back to the horses. If not, come back here and wait for me."

"What're you aimin' to do?"

"Try to convince some varmints it's time to retire."

Having a hard time keeping his balance, the sheriff slowly made his way down the slippery slope and away from Kelly. The marshal watched after him for a moment, then, feeling reasonably sure the sheriff would do as he had been instructed, began to pick his way up the slope to see if he could identify exactly where the Bishops were. He didn't have a long wait in the scrub that lined the edges of the rise like a bald man's fringe. Two figures, standing in the open about twenty feet from the ruins of an adobe building, seemed to be arguing over something.

Just then, a man stumbled into camp leading his skittish bay mare. It was Blackwater Bill DeMotte. Kelly had never actually run across him before, but recognized him from descriptions he'd heard from other lawmen. DeMotte stopped in front of the other two. Of them, Ord Bishop was easily identifiable by the silver conches on his boots. They reflected the lightning flashes like jewels in the sun. Kelly brought the hammer back on his Winchester and prepared to get closer. "They won't get away so easily this time," he whispered under his breath to no one.

"How come you're walking your mount?" Ord said.

"Damned bronco near bucked me off several times when lightnin' hit too close," Blackwater Bill said, wiping at his face in the pelting rain.

"Find a site?"

"Yep. Got the perfect place. They'll be neck deep in the trap before they know what hit 'em."

"Good. Try to get some sleep. We'll leave early." Ord sloshed off as Bill began to unsaddle his storm-shy mare.

Chapter Twenty-six

By now, the rain was coming down in sheets and, for the overweight sheriff, getting around on the hilly, slippery ground had become quite tricky. He had fallen in the mud several times as he moved about the periphery of the Bishops' campsite, trying hard to avoid any contact with the outlaws. Stepping over what he took to be a clump of dry brush, he stumbled, coming down hard on some sharp stones and a couple of cholla burrs. He let out a muffled groan. Just then the "brush" moved. A chill ran through him. He could barely make out a human form. He scooted away quickly, scattering gravel under his heavy boots, pulling his sidearm in the process. His hand shook as he pointed the .38 in the general direction of a shadowy, wriggling figure.

"Wh-who is it?" Potter said in a low, scared voice. "Speak up!" The body he'd fallen over started spitting and choking.

"It's me. Who're you?" came the sputtering reply.

Potter recognized the voice, even from what little he'd heard in his office. "That you, boy?"

"Y-yessir!" Blue squealed.

"Keep your voice down, you damned fool, want to get us all killed?" Potter answered with a growl.

"Who's over there with you, Blue?" called Pooder.

"Sheriff Potter," Blue whispered in a high, squeaky voice. He spit out more of the mouthful of mud he'd acquired when the corpulent sheriff pushed his face into the ground falling over him.

"He come to kill us, too?" Pooder whined.

"If you two ornery fools will hold your tongues, I'll try to cut you loose. But, before I do, I need your word you'll do as I say. Understand?"

"Yessir," Blue said hurriedly.

"Guess that all depends on—" Pooder started.

"Shut your mouth, Pooder!" Blue blurted out in a loud and forceful whisper, determined not to let Pooder take away what looked like their only chance at freedom. "You can count on us, Sheriff, we're with you."

" 'Bout damned time somebody was," Potter mumbled as he slipped his revolver back into its holster.

Forced into a cramped position by the confines of the terrain and the need for cover, he struggled to get a pudgy hand into his pants pocket to secure a small folding knife. After several minutes of effort, he crawled over to Blue, knife in hand. Feeling around in the blackness, he ran a wet hand down the boy's arm to find the rope. Just as he was about to run the blade across the rope, a bolt of lightning shattered the night, leaving him temporarily blinded. He pulled back. That brief flash did, however, reveal that if he'd made the cut the way he was holding the knife, he probably would also have sliced Blue's wrist. He sat back on his heels and waited a moment before trying again, wiping rain out of his eyes with his soaked sleeve.

Blue could tell the sheriff was having trouble seeing well enough to cut him free. "Sir, if I can roll over a little maybe you can cut the rope tying my hands to my feet."

"Okay."

Blue arched his back as much as he could in order to make the rope binding him easier to target. He found little movement possible. But, suddenly, he felt a sharp tug at his binds and heard the snap as Potter successfully freed him from the hog-tied position he'd been forced to suffer for several hours.

The relief was so great he just wanted to lay there in the mud and shout for joy, but that would have been the most foolish thing he could have done. "Thank you," was all he could manage through grateful tears. He ripped at the knot around his ankles with his fingernails. After several seconds, the stubborn knot loosened.

"All right, now help me get the other one free," Potter whispered.

The two of them crawled around a mesquite bush and found Pooder lying in a shallow gully with water flowing rapidly all around him. It was nearly up to his mouth. He was writhing in an attempt to keep from drowning. Another minute and his struggles would have been for nothing. Zebulan Pooder, farm boy, would have just been another body claimed by an unforgiving desert and a flash flood.

Blue scooted alongside his friend and held his head out of the water while Potter slashed at the ropes around Pooder's arms and legs. Free at last, Pooder sputtered, "You know, them Bishops woulda just let me drown if you hadn't come along."

"Likely," said Potter. "Now, stay low and follow me out of here."

There was no hesitation as the three took off like playful otters—half-crawling, half-scurrying, slipping and sliding, in and out of the newly formed rivulets spilling off the ridge, dodging deadly cholla barbs that lurked everywhere, nearly invisible in the dark.

Out of breath from exertion and fear of discovery, Potter held up at the bottom of the ridge. "We'll wait here for a few minutes. Take a rest," Potter said, gasping for air. He sank to his knees. Rushing water filled his boots as it cascaded down the rocky incline. Potter didn't seem to notice.

"You okay, Sheriff?" Blue said.

"Will be. Just need to catch my breath," he said, panting rapidly.

"How'd you find us?" Pooder said.

"Marshal."

"The marshal's with you?"

"He's up there somewhere. Thinkin' of corralin' that bunch

by hisself, I think," he answered, still nearly breathless. "I plan
to let him."

In preparation for the next morning's raid on the gold wagons, J.D. Cartright had carefully wrapped four bottles of nitroglycerin with several layers of dampened cloth and stuffed
them into saddle bags. When the storm started, Hale made
him take them into the closure where the main building had
once stood. By leaning them against one of the crumbling
walls in a niche formed by several fallen adobe bricks, it
seemed the best place for reasonable protection against an
inadvertent shock. It wouldn't take much to set the touchy
explosive off. They couldn't take chances.

 J.D. knew little about nitro. He just sold the stuff. But, since
Johanson had gotten himself shot down in a Charleston street,
Ord had put him in charge of getting it safely to the ambush
site. To this point, he'd done all he could. Now, he settled
down under his slicker, several feet away from the explosives,
trying to get some sleep. But sleep wasn't coming easily.

Kelly watched from behind an outcrop of boulders as the
outlaws tried to find whatever shelter they could find to get
some sleep. Two walls were all that remained of the stage
depot. They afforded what little protection there was against
the storm. No roof, no cover. The four restless horses were
nearby, all tied to the same looming mesquite stand. The
closeness of the lightning and thunder obviously made them
nervous. The storm seemed to be intensifying.

The marshal waited until all four appeared settled. His plan
was to let them wake up staring at the barrel of a Winchester.
He carefully began to make his way down to the encampment.
As he moved, a flash of lightning illuminated the whole area,
making him a perfect target if he were unlucky enough to be
seen. Luck wasn't with him that night. Ord Bishop wasn't
asleep, and he happened to be facing in Kelly's direction when
the strike hit.

Ord jumped to his feet, grabbing his six gun, and started

blasting away in Kelly's direction. He yelled to the others to arm themselves, the law was here!

Kelly dove for cover.

Between wild shots, Ord headed for his horse, dragging his saddle behind him. Though none of Ord's shots came close, Kelly was forced to keep low to the ground as he moved beneath a hail of bullets. He crawled toward an outcropping of boulders and ducked behind him. He rolled around to the far side, came up between the rocks and some brush, and pumped four quick rounds into the camp. Just to keep them honest.

Ord was yanking on his horse's lead, coaxing him into the dark desert and away from the action, using the thick brush for cover. Hale was close behind, throwing shots over his shoulder like a circus trick-shot artist. Blackwater Bill was determined to stand his ground and return fire at his attacker, which he did with two blazing six–guns.

With the whine of ricocheting bullets ringing off the rocks all around him, Kelly moved swiftly, hugging the ground, seeking a better vantage point from which to return fire. He wished he hadn't been where he was when that lightning flashed and gave his position away, but it was too late now for regrets.

J.D. scurried out from under his slicker, raced for the saddle bags of nitro and, slipping and sliding, tugged his .32 free from his soaked coat pocket and began firing at whatever shadows he could make out on the top of the low hill as he, too, headed for his horse. He aimed at nothing in particular, anything and everything. His assessment of his abilities with a firearm were correct, but maybe he'd get lucky.

J.D. made it just past the first adobe wall when a lightning bolt struck the ground only yards away. It was suddenly, and briefly, midday. It gave Kelly that split second he needed to clearly identify a target and fire. He snapped the Winchester to his cheek and squeezed the trigger with unerring accuracy. J.D. Cartright turned out to be that unlucky target. The saddle bags with the carefully packed nitro bottles got in the way of a clean shot through the heart, not that it made any difference.

The night was shattered by the deafening explosion that sent Blackwater Bill flying through the air to land some twenty feet away in a large barrel cactus.

J.D. never knew what had hit him. His drenched sack suit was now nothing more than tatters of smoldering cloth. There was hardly enough left of him to identify, just like those two unfortunate miners back in Desert Belle the night he slipped into the jail with two bottles of the same stuff to free the Bishop brothers. He had been hightailing it out of there when Ord fired a round back into the jail and lit up the sky.

As the storm passed overhead, Kelly, still smarting somewhat from his wound, walked gingerly into the camp, rifle at the ready. The Bishops were long gone by the time he got there, but he had cut the odds in half. Along with J.D., Blackwater Bill DeMotte had also been killed by the fiery blast, aided by quite a few deadly cactus spines that had penetrated deep into his flesh, adding the outlaw's seeping blood to the already water-soaked desert sands.

Two down, two to go.

Chapter Twenty-seven

The storm had passed quickly, stars were once again visible, the sky clear. The air was fresh and clean-smelling. The sudden appearance of the moon gave an eerie, greenish cast to the desert. Kelly stood near where the campfire had been. About all that remained was a tangle of burnt sticks and wet ashes with one, thin ribbon of smoke struggling lazily skyward. He surveyed the scene around him. The two previously standing adobe walls were now nothing more than scattered rubble. Cactus and mesquite that had once stood within a few feet of where the blast took place were now a jumble of green, sticky pulp and a few burned leaves and splintered sticks.

Kelly called out, "Potter! You out there?"

At first he heard nothing. He figured the old fool had probably run off at the first sound of shooting. But after a few seconds he heard voices approaching. He thumbed back the hammer on the Winchester as he dropped to one knee, making himself less of a target as a precaution. From out of the dark shadows came Potter and the two boys stumbling up the slight incline.

"We're here, Marshal," said Potter, taking slow, weary steps toward the camp.

"Good. I see you found them. Everybody okay?" Kelly released the hammer, got to his feet, and cradled the rifle across his chest.

"Just powerful stiff from being bound up like hogs to butcher," Pooder said.

"Sure glad y'all came when you did. A few more minutes and we'd a been coyote bait," said Blue.

"I'm glad to see you're both still in one piece. But you know none of this would have happened if you'd stayed put," Kelly reminded them.

Blue looked at Pooder with a scowl. The sheepish look on Pooder's face told the whole story. Kelly knew he didn't have to press the subject any further.

"I don't suppose either of you overheard the Bishops say where they planned to hit that gold shipment."

"No sir, Marshal. They was right private about givin' out information like that," Blue said.

"You think they'll still try for it without any nitro and short a couple of guns?" Potter said. The doubt on his face told where he stood on the subject. "I'd bet they're half-way to Mexico by now."

"Don't think we can take a chance that they'd give up gettin' their hands on that gold, or what they think will be gold."

"What do you mean?" Potter said, a puzzled look now supplanting the doubtful one.

"I don't think Slaughter plans to send anything to Desert Belle except some empty wagons. And I think he's counting heavily on something happening to those wagons before they ever get to town."

Potter removed his hat and scratched his head. "Afraid you're gonna have to paint me a picture."

"There's no time. You'll have to trust me. We need to find where they plan to hit the wagons, so let's see if we can dig up anything from whatever they left behind, assuming everything isn't just a memory now," Kelly said. He looked Potter straight in the eye to see if he was going to get an argument. Without a word, Potter shrugged and turned away.

The four of them spread out through the camp. Blue picked up a piece of burnt leather with a buckle on it—all that was left of the saddle bags that carried the nitro. Pooder found a small leather satchel that had been burst open at the seams, the papers inside blown about, many snagged on cactus spines. He collected several sheets and handed them to Kelly.

"Maybe that's their plans or something," said Pooder.

"No," said Kelly, "but it's almost as good. It's what's left of Mr. Cartright's order books. And one of these is a note accepting two-hundred dollars for the 'job', and it's signed by Jake Strong. Looks like it was J.D. who paid Strong to try shooting me in my room. J.D. must have figured Ord Bishop would want him to take the initiative. Answers one question, at least."

They continued to kick at debris, occasionally picking up bits and pieces. Blue found the guns the outlaws had taken from the boys. They must have been stashed near the source of the blast because they were no longer usable as weapons. The cylinder of the Remington Rider was blown out of the frame, snapping the post like a toothpick. Pooder's pocket pistol had met a similar fate when the bullets exploded in the chamber from the intense heat, scattering pieces of twisted metal all about.

"Hope we don't need anything to defend ourselves anytime soon," he said, holding the largest surviving piece—the barrel—between two fingers, and staring at it forlornly.

Potter wasn't wandering about with the others. He was staring down at the body of Blackwater Bill. The face of the corpse was splattered with blood. The eyes were open and seemed to be glaring directly at Potter. Potter looked sick.

"We'll hold up here for awhile," said Ord. "We've put enough distance between us and that damned nuisance marshal to sit a spell and rest."

"What do you suppose happened to Bill and J.D.?" Hale asked. "Think they got away?"

"Depends on how far away they were from that nitro when it went up."

"Yeah. Well, what do we do now? Guess we can forget the gold. Maybe head south to Mexico, huh?" Hale said.

"Forget the gold? Hell no! We're gettin' that gold, and that's all there is to it!"

"How? There's just the two of us. We ain't no match for all them guards." Hale was frowning at his brother as if he'd lost his mind.

"How many times have you played cards with me?" Ord asked.

"That's a fool question. A bunch, I reckon."

"How many times did you win?"

"Can't recall none. You're just powerful lucky. What's that got to do with how we walk up and take over a wagon train with only two guns?"

"It's called having an ace in the hole. I always have one."

"You sayin' you was cheatin' every time you sat down to a card game? You son of a bitch, you'd steal from your own brother?"

"Chalk it up to experience, little brother." Ord turned to reach into his saddle bags and pull out a package wrapped in brown paper. He held the package up defiantly. "Here's our ace in the hole."

"What the hell's in there?"

"Dynamite. Four sticks of it. It won't work as well as the nitro, and we'll have to change our plans a little, but it'll get us a handsome chunk of that gold, just not all of it."

"So, how we goin' to do that?"

"We'll separate about thirty yards apart. When the first wagon gets to me, I'll light a short fuse and throw it in the road far enough ahead of 'em so the horses ain't killed. When you hear the explosion, you'll do the same near the second wagon. While they're all trying to figure out what the hell's happenin', I'll shoot the driver and guards on the first wagon. You'll have to detain the others, keepin' them pinned down with the other two sticks of powder and some well-aimed gunfire while I take over the first wagon and drive it into the brush. Those guards will be so busy savin' their hides, they won't bother comin' after me."

"What happens when the rest of them figure out they only have one man left to contend with?"

"You get the hell outta there and join up with me at the place we originally talked about," Ord said. He dug his heels into his horse's ribs and slapped at the reins. The plan was set. Hale wasn't given time to ask any more questions. Ord had determined it was time to do what they did best.

"Can't spend any more time here," Kelly said. "We'll have to take a chance that you're right, Sheriff; we'll strike out for Smoky Ridge."

"I'll get our horses," Potter said as he ambled off toward where he and Kelly had left them tied.

"Did you happen to see the boys' horses anywhere?"

"Probably left them back in town and carried them two over the rumps of their own horses," Potter said.

"Cartright's and DeMotte's horses ought to be somewhere around here. So, boys, unless you're prepared for a long walk, you better start lookin'," Kelly said.

Pooder and Blue hurried into the brush in opposite directions. Blue came upon J.D.'s horse almost immediately. The gray mare was standing at the bottom of the hill, her reins still wrapped around the branch she'd been tied to, although the rest of the mesquite tree was long gone. With a calm, reassuring voice, Blue was able to catch the mare, mount, and coax her into a slow walk back up the hill.

Pooder was having his usual luck—which was no luck at all. All he had found were low-hanging cholla burrs that seemed to sneak up on him in the dark at every turn. His pants were torn and his skin scratched and bloody. After a short search, he decided to give up and go back to the camp site. It was safer there.

When he got there, the others were mounted and ready, just waiting for him to return.

"Couldn't find the other one," he whined. "I'll just stay here till you come back for me."

"I don't plan to come back this way. Better climb up behind your friend. That'll be preferable to walkin' outta here. You'd only make it about halfway to Desert Belle before you came up number one on some buzzard's menu," said Kelly. "I can just see some Mescalero sneakin' up on an enemy while wearin' those overalls of yours."

The imagery wasn't wasted on the boy.

Blue quickly leaned over to lend a hand up. With a shudder at the thought of dying in the desert, Pooder wasted no time getting settled on the gray mare. They started out single file behind Kelly, bound for Smoky Ridge and a showdown.

With the two boys bringing up the rear, Pooder seemed to have some time on his hands. Time to think. As far as Blue was concerned, that was when Pooder was the most dangerous. He remembered his mother saying something about idle hands and the devil, but he couldn't recall the exact saying. He did know it probably applied precisely to Zeb Pooder.

"Got any idea what happens when we get to Smoky Ridge?" Potter asked. He seemed edgy, reluctant to be heading into a certain gunfight with men who'd as soon shoot a sheriff down in the dirt as look at him. The idea of being a target didn't sit well with the sheriff. Especially since he made such an easy target.

"No. We'll wait and see when we get there."

"Great," mumbled Potter under his breath, "now I've got to wait and see how I'm goin' to get my butt shot off."

Chapter Twenty-eight

T he glow of a fresh new dawn was just presenting itself over the rim of the mountains to the east. Nearly all signs of the evening's storm had vanished, dry creek beds were returning to their previous state, the parched ground crunched underfoot, nearly as dry as ever.

When Kelly and Potter arrived at the base of Smoky Ridge, they dismounted and prepared to climb to the top, the most obvious vantage point from which to survey the surrounding area. From there, Kelly hoped to spot the Bishops hunkering down in wait for the wagons from the Gilded Lily to roll into their ambush.

Having lagged behind from riding double on a strange horse, Pooder and Blue caught up just as the lawmen were about to ascend the hill. Piedmont Kelly turned to them as Blue tugged awkwardly at the rope lead in an attempt to get the horse to stop.

"You boys stay here, out of sight, and keep quiet," Kelly admonished. "You can watch our horses."

"Yessir," said Blue as he slid off the gray mare's bare back. Pooder followed with a scowl. Blue caught sight of a pensive look on Pooder's face, and was certain he was thinking up some new scheme. Blue wanted no part of it, whatever it was. He took the reins handed to him by the sheriff and the marshal and walked all three horses to where he could tie them securely to a mesquite limb.

Rifle in hand, Kelly stooped to make a low profile and began carefully to pick his way to the top of the point on Smoky Ridge. Potter slipped and slid, nearly loosing his balance every few feet, trying to keep up with the younger and more agile marshal.

At the summit, they were able to stay out of sight behind an outcropping of several boulders. They settled down to scour the desert below for signs of men or horses. Directly in front of them, about three-quarters of a mile away was a tight horseshoe bend. It was the place Potter had said would be a likely spot to find the Bishops waiting.

Kelly felt a wave of anger come over him as his eyes fell to the small clearing at the base of a nearby rise just off the road where he'd nearly lost his life, lying face down in the sand, slowly bleeding to death from Potter's bullet.

He chewed his lip as he suppressed his first impulse—to bring the rifle swiftly around and blow Potter into the next world. His anger was brief. It passed quickly as reason took control. He knew he'd better concentrate on the business at hand. Any further dealings he might have on the subject of the incompetent sheriff could wait.

A flash of brightness, possibly sunlight glinting off a gun barrel, caught the marshal's attention. He watched the swale where the light had caught his eye, looking for signs of movement. About ten yards behind where he'd seen the flash, he spotted a horse grazing on dry grass. He recognized the mare as the same one he'd seen Ord Bishop leading out of camp in his haste to escape capture the night before.

A moment later, Ord's fancy boots gave him away. They sparkled in the early sun as he squatted behind some brush. Off in the far distance a trail of dust was rising from the desert. *Here come the wagons*, Kelly thought. No time for any elaborate planning.

Piedmont Kelly was ready to make his move. "I've spotted Ord. It's time." He pushed himself out of his crouched position and started down the back of the incline so as not to be seen. Ord Bishop had already gotten one chance to see him before he was ready, he wouldn't get a second.

"Okay, Marshal. Good luck. I'll stay right here and keep an eye out," Potter said.

"Like hell."

Kelly turned, took hold of Potter's shirt front and pulled him abruptly to his feet. Potter started to protest, then thought better of it. Reluctantly, he trailed the marshal to the bottom. Blue stood up as they approached.

"You two stay here. We're goin' after them," Kelly said. Blue just nodded his understanding of the order.

After the two lawmen disappeared into the brush, Pooder came out from behind a rock and joined Blue. "They gone?" he asked.

"Yes. Why?"

"Got me a plan. We're goin' to make us some more money," he said, puffed up like a peacock and grinning from ear to ear.

"Now hold on, the marshal said to stay put, and this time, I think he'd as soon skin us if we don't do what he says," Blue insisted.

"Not if we was to help. Lord knows he's goin' up against a couple a mighty tough outlaws. That sheriff is worthless. Bet the marshal wouldn't refuse another gun."

"First off, we don't got no guns. Second, he said stay put in a voice that I took to mean just that," Blue said. "I'm stayin', and that's that."

"That's okay by me. Then I won't have to share my reward," Pooder said, turning away.

"What reward?"

"Got to be a reward for them Bishops, don't there?"

"Say, what you got in the pocket of them overalls? You look all lumpy," Blue asked.

A wry grin overtook the young pig farmer's face as he stuck his hand into the deep side pocket and pulled out a silver-plated revolver. Blue's eyes opened wide.

"Wh-where'd you come up with that?" he sputtered.

"It was lyin' right near to the body of that man got blowed

into the cactus plant. I didn't figure he'd be needin' it no more, so I liberated it." Pooder held the revolver out in front of him, twirling it around his index finger, trying to look every inch the experienced gunfighter.

Blue buried his head in his hands. "I can't believe this," he mumbled.

"C'mon, we're gettin' in on the action." Pooder didn't wait for an answer. Instead, he quickly disappeared into the brush, following the trail the bulky sheriff had left. It was the easy one to track.

Blue threw up his hands and went after his friend, knowing full well that disaster was bound to be nearby. He didn't have long to wait.

He was about ten yards behind Pooder when he heard a voice say, "Well, well, what have we here?" It was Hale Bishop. Pooder had stumbled onto where the outlaw was hidden in the brush.

As Blue got closer, he could see Pooder waving the newly acquired six-shooter out in front of him. He was shakily gripping the weapon in both hands, struggling with all his might to cock the hammer using one thumb on top of the other. The revolver was much larger and heavier than the one he was used to, and that, together with surging fear, found his thumbs repeatedly slipping off the hammer. A continuous flow of curses flew from his lips as if that would help stave off the inevitable.

Hale just stared at him with a sneering grin on his weather-beaten face. He laughed aloud as he went for his own sidearm. Just as he raised it to shoot the badly shaken young fool he faced, another voice came from the brush off to Hale's side.

"Throw it away, Hale," shouted Sheriff Potter, panting and wheezing. Hale spun around and fired. Potter's gun went off simultaneously as he went down hard on one knee with a bullet in his chest.

Hale staggered back for a moment, then, holding a shattered right arm close to his side with his left hand, turned and stumbled off. Unable to retain any grip in his gun hand, he dropped his .44 Remington as blood oozed from between his fingers and dripped on the ground, leaving a trail behind him.

Blue ran up to Pooder, who was standing with a dazed look on his face, tears streaming down his cheeks. He was shaking like he'd been stricken with a palsy.

"H-he could have killed me without another thought. I was a dead man." Pooder whimpered. "I'm giving up guns, yes I am, and you can believe it." He threw the revolver into the dirt.

Showing neither belief in Pooder's declaration nor sympathy for his close call with death, Blue just shook his head, then turned as he heard a pitiful groan in time to see Potter collapse on the rocky soil, his wrinkled old shirt now covered with bright red.

"Sheriff, you been shot!" Blue cried out. "Pooder, he's been shot!" Pooder was in another world. He couldn't hear anything but the knocking of his own knees.

Blue cried out, "You hang on, Sheriff. I'll go get help." He took off at a dead run toward where he figured the marshal would most likely be. "You stay with him, Pooder," he called back for no real reason. Pooder hadn't moved an inch.

Kelly could just make out where Ord Bishop was settled in behind a tangle of silver dollar cactus and blue paloverde. He crept quietly to within eight or ten feet, and prepared to get the drop on the unsuspecting outlaw. He held the Winchester just slightly out in front of him, moving it slowly from side to side as he surveyed the area. Just as he was about to make his move, he heard an unexpected sound. Hale Bishop came from nowhere, lumbering through the brush.

Ord was already agitated by the sound of gunfire coming from where his brother was supposed to have been. He mumbled something about how if that fool brother of his fouled up this robbery by plugging some ratter or gopher, he'd shoot the son of a gun himself. He was completely caught off guard by what happened next.

Surprised by the sight of someone crashing into the clearing behind him, Ord instinctively spun around and fired two quick shots in that direction. Hale stumbled out and fell dead at his brother's feet, a second and third bullet hole now piercing his body. The last one, offered up by his own brother, had hit him right in the heart, killing him instantly.

Ord looked with shock at what he'd done. He bent down to be certain that those pleading eyes were, indeed, actually empty of all life. There was no doubt. His head slumped to his chest.

Kelly decided to take that opportunity to brace the last remaining Bishop brother. He stepped from behind a mesquite tree and shouted, "Ord! Ord Bishop! Give it up!"

Startled by Kelly's voice, the outlaw reacted quickly, but not quickly enough.

Ord's shot went into the dirt in front of him. He'd been a fraction of a second behind the marshal's quicker reaction. Kelly's bullets found their mark right where he'd planned: two, side-by-side holes decorated Ord's shirt front. Ord Bishop died face down in the desert sand that very instant, only a few feet from his brother.

Just then, Blue came running up, skidding to a halt at the sight of the two dead Bishop brothers. He swallowed hard several times before he could speak. "Mister Marshal, the sheriff's been shot bad," he struggled to say.

For a time, Kelly's mind replayed the past week, the doubts about the Bishops really being dead in the jail blast, and all that had brought him to this fateful moment. Finally, realizing that Blue was standing there tugging at his shirt sleeve, Kelly shook off his reminiscent daze. "What?"

"The sheriff's been shot. Better come."

"Okay, Blue, lead the way."

Upon reaching Potter, Kelly instantly recognized the seriousness of his wound. The bullet had missed his heart, but not by much. And from look of the blood bubbling out of the gaping hole, he was sure a lung had been punctured. The sheriff had slipped into unconsciousness.

Kelly told Blue to go find his horse, bring the blanket from behind his saddle, and cover Potter with it.

"Try to stop the bleeding with my scarf, and keep him

warm. I'll stop the wagons and try to get some help." He handed Blue the scarf he'd untied from around his neck, and with long, hurried strides, headed for the road some twenty yards away. He could hear the approaching rumble of horse and wagon.

Chapter Twenty-nine

T he two wagons were coming fast. Kelly ran into the road waving his arms, his Winchester held high. The lead driver was Molly. When she saw the marshal, she reined back hard on the team, stiff-legging the brake at the same time. The back end of her wagon slid sideways on the gravel, nearly leaving the roadbed. Dust nearly swallowed them for a moment as the wagons finally came to a halt.

Still having to hold the reins taught, Molly tried to calm the skittish and well-lathered team as they pranced in place.

"What is it, Marshal?" she asked. "Bandits up ahead?"

"Not any more," he said, "they're all dead."

"Damn, we don't have to run that gauntlet, after all," she answered with a sigh of relief. She eased off the brake, finally able to control the team with just the reins. "I had a terrible feeling something was going to happen just around nearly every bend we came to. I'm thankful you were here."

"Makes us even. Where are your guards? How come Slaughter only sent a driver with each wagon?"

"He said we'd have a better chance of bein' left alone if we looked like we weren't carryin' anything of value. I'll admit, the plan scared me right from the beginning." She pulled up the red kerchief that hung around her neck to wipe the sweat from her face.

"Molly, I need to have a look at that load you're carrying," Kelly said.

"Uh, well I don't know, Marshal. If Slaughter found out I let someone open those boxes before we got to the bank . . ."

Kelly walked closer. He eyed the driver on the second wagon. The man was sitting calmly, leaning forward with his forearms on his knees, loosely holding the reins, his rifle leaned against the side of the foot-well. He made no attempt to reach for it. Kelly glanced back at Molly.

"What if I told you I don't think there's any gold in there?"

"No gold? Ridiculous. Slaughter himself supervised the loading. Of course there's gold. What you said back in town just can't be true."

"One way to find out. If I'm wrong, there's been no harm."

The other driver spoke up, "Let him look, Molly. Sooner we get this settled, the sooner we get to town with this load."

"Okay, Marshal. Go ahead." Molly wrapped the reins around the high brake handle and lifted a leg over the side to climb down. The marshal met her at the back of the wagon. She loosed the pins holding the tailgate. It fell with a thud. Kelly groaned a little as he pulled himself onto the wagon bed, still sore from his wound. A crowbar lay on the bed near the first box. He jammed it under the lid and yanked up hard. The lid gave way easily and slid off to one side. Kelly looked at the contents with a frown.

"Well . . ." Molly prodded.

"Have a look for yourself."

"I'll take your word for it. What's in there?"

The other driver hopped down from his own rig, came over to Molly's wagon and hauled himself up beside Kelly. The look on his face was a mixture of surprise and anger. "Rocks! Ain't nothing but rocks!" he yelled. "We been riskin' our fool necks for a load of rocks!"

Molly shook her head from side to side as she stared at her feet. She kicked at a rock in the road.

"What's all this mean, Marshal?" she said, with a catch in her voice.

"I'll tell you later. Right now, I need another favor. Up the

road a-piece you'll find Sheriff Potter with the boys. They said
he's pretty well shot up. See if you can get him to the doctor
in town. He may not make it. Took one in the chest and he's
bleeding badly." Kelly jumped from the wagon, reached up
and pulled the box of rocks out of the wagon and let it crash
to the ground, spilling its contents on the road.

He strode purposefully to his horse and quickly mounted.

"Hey, where are you goin'?" Molly asked, with hands on
her hips like she thought he ought to be staying with them.

"There's still one piece missing to all this. I need a word
with your employer. A serious word. See you back in town."
Kelly slapped the reins and the big gelding leapt into a dead
run down the road toward the Gilded Lily, scattering gravel
like small explosions with every lunging step.

Kelly's hurried arrival at the main gate to the mine property
drew considerable attention. Men working on machinery or
loading crates onto wagons stopped to watch as the marshal
passed by, bringing his horse to a halt in front of Slaughter's
office, and pulling his carbine from its saddle scabbard.

Two rough looking characters with low-slung six-shooters
sat on chairs leaning back against the whipsaw siding of the
porch. When Kelly dismounted, one of the men got up and
went inside. In a moment he returned, motioned for the other
to follow him, and the two stepped off the porch, never taking
their eyes off the marshal.

Just to make sure the word got around he wasn't there for
a social visit, Kelly cocked the hammer on the Winchester as
he stood, straight as a ramrod, feet apart, rifle across his chest.
Waiting.

Moments later the door creaked open and Slaughter stepped
onto the porch. He was armed with a .44 Colt that sat up high
and at an angle on his gunbelt. Cross–draw style. His hands
hung nervously at his sides.

"What can I do for you, Marshal?" he said.

Out of the corner of his eye, Kelly could see that the two
gunmen had taken up positions several yards away and to

either side of him. They had him in a cross-fire if things got hot.

"You can oblige me by easing that Colt out of its holster with your left hand, very slowly. Then you can drop it on the porch and have someone saddle a horse for you. You're coming back to Desert Belle with me," Kelly said. His steel blue eyes never left King Slaughter as he awaited the man's next move.

"And just why would I do that?" Slaughter said with a wry smile.

"First off, I'm takin' you in for the murder of Deputy Sheriff Ben Satterfield."

"Hogwash! How do you intend to prove that?"

"When I was laid up those couple a days, I remember noticing a double eagle on your watch chain. You aren't wearing it today. What happened to it?

Unconsciously, Slaughter's hand dropped to the empty chain that crossed from one vest pocket to another. "The fob probably just fell off somewhere or another. I'll find it one of these days."

Kelly reached into his own vest pocket and pulled out the double-eagle. He tossed it in the dirt in front of him. "I'll save you the trouble of looking," he said.

"Wh-where'd you find it?"

"It was in Ben Satterfield's dead fist. He must have lunged for you just before you shot him in the chest, grabbing the fob on the way down. He gripped it so tight, in death it left an easily identifiable mark on his hand. It's all the evidence I'll need to convict you of murder. Now, drop that gun."

King Slaughter just mumbled something about telling Potter never to let Satterfield in his sight again, but made no move to comply with the marshal's order. From a distance, Kelly heard the rattle of a wagon being driven hard and coming closer. He didn't take his eyes off Slaughter when the wagon came to a halt not far away. He heard the sound of footsteps on the hardpan behind him.

Slaughter frowned at the sight of the two wagons as they

came to a rattling halt several yards away. "What the hell you doin' back here?" he yelled.

"I feel obliged to answer that one, Slaughter," Kelly said. "Somehow, there didn't seem to be anyone left alive out there to hold up your little stone-haulin' convoy. Your attempt to drive one last stake into the heart of Desert Belle has failed. The town may not be able to survive on its own, only time will tell, but at least it won't have to suffer any more of your broken promises just so you can have revenge."

"It ain't over, yet. You'll not be leaving here alive, Marshal. You're out–numbered and out–gunned." Slaughter smiled contemptuously.

"Maybe, but you'll be the first to go, no matter what happens to me. I'll shoot you first and let what takes place next come as it will," Kelly said. His voice was one of cold determination. Slaughter shifted nervously from one foot to another. The air was charged with the electricity of nerves stretched to their limits.

Kelly thought he detected a slight movement from off to one side. One of Slaughter's hired guns, he figured. He readied his move. Then a voice broke the silence. A very familiar voice.

"If I were you, Ortez, I'd reconsider touching that Colt," said Molly. Her warning was followed by the sound of several hammers being cocked. "Same goes for you, Stringer."

"Looks like it's just you and me, Slaughter. What'll it be? Your choice." The brim of Kelly's Stetson drooped slightly in front, shading his eyes from the intense sun. But Slaughter would have no trouble seeing in that steely stare that Kelly was not in a bargaining mood.

Time seemed at a stand-still, demanding action before it could resume.

King Slaughter made his decision in the blink of an eye. His hand went for the Colt with an unexpected quickness. He was fast for a man more used to bookkeeping than gun-play. The hammer came back in one fluid movement as the six-gun cleared the holster.

One echoing shot shattered the silence. One single, unerring

bullet sped to its target. The shock on King Slaughter's face
told the whole story as, having barely cleared leather, he was
slammed against the wall with the force of a sledge hammer,
a gaping crater in the center of his forehead. His dead body
slid slowly down the wall to a sitting position, head drooped,
leaving a broad trail of blood on the wood behind him.

King Slaughter's body sat slumped over like a rag doll. He
had murdered Satterfield in order to balance his ledger—an
eye for an eye. But he had gone much further than that as the
hatred in his heart had poisoned his mind with the desire to
carry his vendetta even further: to also murder a town. He
paid the price for his ill-considered plans with a single bullet
from a Winchester .44.

"Wrong choice," mumbled Kelly as he turned to see Molly,
Pooder, Blue, and several other men with weapons aimed at
the two hired guns. "Gentlemen, I'd say your services have
been terminated. I hear they're looking for your type over in
Texas. Be a good idea to start now."

Ortez and Stringer both nodded acceptance of the generous
offer to leave. They were mounted and out of camp before
Kelly could reach Molly and the boys to thank them for their
help.

"I'm surprised to see you here, Molly, but pleased," he said.
"I sure thank you."

"I figured we had a better doc out here than they have in
town, so I thought to bring Potter to the Lily. Then we seen
you in what appeared to be a tense situation. Figured you
could use a hand."

"You figured right."

"By the way, the sheriff was dead soon after we left for the
Lily. Sorry."

"So am I. Potter wasn't much of a lawman, but I didn't
want to see him gunned down by the likes of Hale Bishop."

"Wow!" said Pooder, "I never seen nobody as fast with a
rifle as you, Marshal."

"Yeah, that guy never had a chance," said Blue.

"He had a chance, Blue," said Kelly, "he could have surrendered and faced a trial. Maybe, to a man like King Slaughter, this way's better than waitin' for a rope."

"What was the idea of all them boxes of rocks?" the other wagon driver asked. "Why all the pretense of their bein' gold in them?"

"Slaughter had such a hatred for Desert Belle and Ben Satterfield for his son's death, I guess he snapped. When he heard the Bishops had escaped, he sent his man, Ortez, to make contact and let them think he was willing to be their eyes and ears for a price—to tell them the mine was going to make a big gold shipment. Slaughter knew they'd take the bait. He sent you out without guards to make sure the Bishops took the wagons without much trouble. You two were expendable. He figured without that shipment, it would be the last blow to the town, and Desert Belle would shrivel up and die. The Bishops would get blamed, he'd collect a handsome sum from his insurance company, and still have all his gold. Gold that never left the Lily."

"Even after we talked about it back in town, I found it hard to believe Slaughter could do something so evil," said Molly.

"I'll be damned," was all the other driver could manage. "My life came within five minutes of bein' over out there! I'll just be damned!"

Chapter Thirty

"**M**arshal!" yelled Molly McQueen as she trudged up the hill toward Mrs. Dunham's boarding house. Marshal Piedmont Kelly was busy stuffing his rolled-up extra set of clothes into one of his saddle bags. Blue and Pooder were sitting silently on the steps of the old porch, elbows on their knees, chins in their hands like twin statues. Their expressions were those of lost puppies. Before the sheriff died, he had told them there would be no reward for Big Al Barton. The reward had been posted by a bank that was no longer in business, the victim of one too many such robberies.

Mrs. Dunham sat humming to herself in one of the two drab wicker chairs on the porch.

"What is it?" Kelly said turning abruptly.

"Couldn't let you go without so much as a fare-thee-well after all you done," Molly said as she came to a panting halt. Shaking her head, she bent over and placed her hands on her knees to catch her breath. "I'm gettin' too old for such nonsense. A woman my age ought to be eyein' the first rocking chair she comes to instead of runnin' up hills like some fool goat."

"Well, it was nice of you to come see me off, Molly. Thanks."

"Come on up here and take a load off, Molly," Mrs. Dunham said. "Got a nice rocker up here ought to fit you fine. Perfect for two old war-horses like us."

"Obliged," Molly said as she started up the weathered steps. A muffled groan seemed to escape her lips with each move. She plopped into the chair with a sigh of relief, still breathing heavily.

Finally packed and ready for his ride back to Ft. Huachuca, Kelly patted his horse on the neck as he walked around the big gelding to say his goodbyes.

From down the street the rattling sounds of a buckboard being driven hard attracted everyone's attention.

"Looks like the banker, Franklin. Seems in one powerful hurry," said Mrs. Dunham as she squinted to identify who it was in the noisily approaching conveyance. A small dust storm whirled about as the driver yanked furiously at the reins in an effort to bring the well-lathered horse to a halt in front of the house.

"Lordy, Mr. Franklin, must be the devil himself chasin' you to be torturin' that poor horse in such a heat," Mrs. Dunham scolded.

"Got somethin' important to say to Molly, Ma'am. Sorry to disturb you." Mr. Franklin pulled a long, white handkerchief from his inside coat pocket. He began mopping his forehead and neck like he was attempting to put out a brush fire. He jumped down from the buckboard, leaving it standing in the middle of the street, and hurried to where he could talk more easily to those on the porch. "Molly, I got a proposition for you."

"Me?" Molly said, her eyebrows twisted into a quizzical furrow. "You sure you ain't got me confused with some other Molly?"

" 'Course I'm sure. Can't be more'n one of you, can there?" puffed the banker.

"Heavens, I hope not. Okay, fire away," Molly said with a shrug.

Banker Franklin first tipped his bowler hat to Mrs. Dunham, who returned the courtesy with a nod. She then continued rocking back and forth slowly. Franklin, still wiping perspiration from his face cleared his throat.

"Seems the late Mr. King Slaughter, him bein' the owner of the Gilded Lily and all, passed without a will, and without any kinfolk. In addition, he owed the bank a sizable sum on monies loaned to him as working capital. And he hadn't been makin' his payments for the past two years or so, so the interest on top of the principal has grown to a tidy sum, all of which is in the form of a secured note."

"Mister, if you're askin' me for a loan to get Slaughter's debt paid, you've come callin' on empty pockets," Molly said, halting Franklin's story with a blustery interruption. "Besides, I don't rightly know what all them big words mean, anyway."

"To start with, it means the bank has gone into the minin' business by default," said Franklin.

"Sounds like all those men out there will still have jobs. That's good," said Kelly.

"Won't have if they're depending on me to run that operation. I can keep the books in order, but I don't know a whit about pullin' gold out of the ground." Franklin wiped at his brow more. "But then, that's what I'm here about. Molly, you been around that mine longer than anybody I can think of, and you get along with the men. You got their respect, too, for bein' a hard worker and honest."

"Jus' what are you gettin' at, Franklin?" Molly said with a squint and a scowl.

"Just that the bank's Board of Directors and I talked it over and we think you'd make a darned fine manager for the Lily. What say? I guarantee we'll make you a fair offer." Franklin took his hat off and held it in front of him.

Molly's mouth dropped. She looked first at Mrs. Dunham, then at Kelly. "Uh, I don't, uh—" she fumbled for words.

"That is one fine idea, Franklin," Kelly jumped in. He slapped the banker on the back, then looked up at Molly who still showed disbelief that anybody would consider her for such an important job. "With someone as dedicated as Molly whippin' things into shape out there, this town's likely to get back on its feet."

"My thoughts exactly," said Franklin. "So, what about it, Molly?"

Molly looked around at the several faces all waiting to see what she would say. After a moment, she turned to Pooder and Blue and said, "Boys, what do you think? Interested in comin' to work for an old worn-out muleskinner?"

"Us? Jobs?" cried Blue. "You really mean it?"

"Yeah, you really gonna give us work?" Pooder jumped in with eyes as wide as saucers. "And we'd get paid actual wages?"

"That's the deal, boys. You two come help me, I'll take the job."

Pooder and Blue grabbed each other by the shoulders, accompanied by wide smiles. "Yes!"

"There's your answer, Mr. Franklin. I reckon I've just made my first decision as your new manager," Molly said.

Franklin sighed deeply, as if a great weight had been lifted from him. He wiped at his face once again before returning the handkerchief to his pocket. "Thank you, Molly. The whole town thanks you."

There were enough smiles in the group to light up a party. Kelly tipped his hat to the ladies as he mounted his horse. "Stay out of trouble, boys," he said. "If you can."

"I'll see to it," said Blue as he waved to the marshal. Pooder punched him on the shoulder at the inference he needed watching over.

For all of King Slaughter's scheming, Desert Belle wouldn't die today.